black
friday

Other titles available in Vintage Crime/Black Lizard

By David Goodis

Shoot the Piano Player

By Jim Thompson

After Dark, My Sweet
The Getaway
The Grifters
A Hell of a Woman
Pop. 1280

By Charles Willeford

The Burnt Orange Heresy
Pick-Up

By Charles Williams

The Hot Spot

black friday

david goodis

VINTAGE CRIME / **BLACK LIZARD**

vintage books • a division of random house, inc. • new york

First Vintage Crime/Black Lizard Edition, October 1990

Library of Congress Cataloging-in-Publication Data
Goodis, David, 1917–1967.
Black Friday/by David Goodis—1st Vintage crime/Black Lizard ed.
p.   cm.—(Vintage crime/Black Lizard)
ISBN 0-679-73255-1
I. Title.   II. Series.
PS3513.O499B55   1990
813'.52—dc20   90-50249   CIP

Manufactured in the United States of America
10 9 8 7 6 5 4 3 2 1

black
friday

January cold came in from two rivers, formed four walls around Hart and closed in on him. He told himself an overcoat was imperative. He looked up and down Callohill Street and saw an old guy coming toward him and the old guy featured a big overcoat and big, heavy work shoes. The overcoat came nearer and Hart worked his way into an alley and waited. He was shivering and he could feel the cold eating into his chest and tearing away at his spine. He came out of the alley as the old guy walked past, and he was behind him. The street was empty. He moved up on the old guy and then noticed how the old guy was bent and the overcoat was old and torn. The old guy would have a hard time getting another overcoat.

Hart turned and walked down Callohill Street. He pulled up the collar of his chocolate-brown flannel suit and told himself a lot of good that did. He turned around again and walked toward Broad Street, and he was hating Philadelphia.

The cold was even worse on Broad Street. From the east it brought an icy flavor from the Delaware. From the west it carried a mean grey frost from the Schuylkill. Hart had been brought up in a warm climate and besides that he was a skinny man and he couldn't stand this cold weather.

He looked south on Broad Street and the big clock on City Hall said six-twenty. It was already getting dark and lights were showing in store windows here and there. Hart put his hands in his trousers pockets and continued north on Broad Street. Then he took his hand out of his left pocket and looked at three quarters, a dime, a nickel and three pennies. That was all he had and he needed an overcoat. He needed a meal and a place to stay and he could use a cigarette. He thought maybe it would be a good idea to walk across Broad and keep on walking until he reached the Delaware River and then take a fast dive and put an end to the whole thing.

He grinned. Just thinking about it made him feel better. It made him realize that as long as he was alive he'd get along somehow. He could hope for a break.

The cold hit again from four sides, got inside him and began to freeze there. He walked on fighting the cold. He passed a store window with a mirror border and stood looking at himself. The flannel suit was still in fairly good shape and that helped some. The collar of the white shirt was grey at the edges and that wasn't so good. He had a mania for clean white shirts. That was something else he needed, a few shirts and underwear and socks. It was a pity he had to get off that train in such a hurry. In a few months or so the railroad would be auctioning his suitcase and his things.

He stood there looking in the mirror, and the cold beat into his back. He needed a haircut. His pale blond hair was wisping around his ears. And he needed a shave. His eyes were pale grey and there were dark shadows under his eyes. He was getting older. In another month he'd be thirty-four.

He smiled sadly at the poor thing in the mirror, the poor skinny thing. Once he had owned a yacht.

It was really dark now and he told himself he better get a move on. He walked on another block and then stopped in front of a clothing store. A sign in the window announced a sale. A prematurely bald man was arranging garments in the window. Hart walked into the store.

The salesman smiled eagerly at Hart.

Hart said, "I'd like to see an overcoat."

"Why, certainly," the salesman said. "We've got a lot of fine ones."

"I only want one," Hart said.

"Why, certainly," the salesman said again. He started toward a rack and then turned and stared at Hart. "How come you're stuck without an overcoat in this weather?"

"I'm careless," Hart said. "I don't take care of myself."

The salesman was looking at Hart's turned-up coat collar.

Hart said, "Do you want to sell me an overcoat?"

"Why, certainly," the salesman said. "What kind would you like?"

"The warm kind."

The salesman took a coat from a hanger. "Just feel that fleece. Try it on. You never wore anything like that in all your life. Just feel it."

Hart got into the coat. It was much too large. He took it off and handed it back to the salesman.

"What's the matter?" the salesman said.

"It's too small," Hart said.

The salesman handed Hart another coat, saying, "Try that on and see how it fits."

Hart got into the coat. It was a fair fit.

"There's your coat," the salesman said.

Hart ran his fingers along the bright green fleece. He said, "How much?"

"Thirty-nine seventy-five," the salesman said. "And it's a buy. I'm telling you it's a real buy. You can see for yourself, it's a buy." The salesman whirled, and as if he was summoning help for a drowning man he waved an arm and yelled, "Harry, come over here!"

The prematurely bald man came out of the window and walked across the store.

The salesman said, "Harry, come here and take a look at this coat."

Harry put long fingers into his trousers pockets and looked at the overcoat and began to nod solemnly.

"That's what I call an overcoat," the salesman said.

"It's one of the specials, isn't it?" Harry said.

"Why, certainly," the salesman said. "Why, certainly its one of the specials."

"How much did you say it was?" Hart asked.

"Thirty-nine seventy-five," the salesman said. "And if you can get another value like that any place in town, you go ahead. You go right ahead and see if you can find another overcoat like that in town. A genuine Lapama fleece for only thirty-nine seventy-five. I'm telling you I don't know how we stay in business."

Hart frowned dubiously and looked down at the front of the coat. Then, as his head was lowered he brought his gaze up and he saw the salesman winking at Harry.

The salesman said, "Harry, if he doesn't buy this coat you put it in the window with one of the big price tags and five will get you fifty we sell it in ten minutes."

5

"Do you mean what you're saying?" Hart asked.

"Why, certainly," the salesman said. "Do you realize what fine fleece that is? If you don't take that overcoat you'll never forgive yourself."

"All right," Hart said. "I'll take it." He walked toward the door.

"That'll be thirty-nine seventy-five," the salesman said. He was walking behind Hart, and then he got excited as Hart moved faster, and he said, "Hey, listen—"

Hart opened the door and ran out.

There were three customers in the small taproom on Twelfth Street off Race. As Hart came in the three customers turned and looked at him and the man behind the bar kept on wiping a glass. Hart walked into the lavatory and took off the coat and tore off the size slip and the price ticket. With the coat over his shoulder he came out of the lavatory and went up to the bar and ordered a beer. He was two-thirds finished with the beer when a policeman entered the taproom and stood there in the doorway examining the four faces and then walked slowly toward Hart.

Hart looked up, holding the glass close to his mouth.

The policeman gestured toward the bright green coat. "Where did you get that?"

"In a store," Hart said.

"Where?"

"I think it was Atlantic City. Or it might have been Albuquerque."

"Are you trying to be smart?"

"Yes," Hart said.

"You stole that coat, didn't you?"

"Sure," Hart said, and he tossed the beer into the policeman's eyes, going forward as the policeman let out a yell going backward, and he was past the policeman, hearing the excitement behind him as he ran out.

Holding tightly to the coat over his arm he ran down Twelfth Street and turned east on Race. Then he went up Eleventh and ran down an alley. In the middle of the alley he came to a stop and he got into the overcoat and leaned against a wall of splintered wood and breathed heavily. He was trying to decide where he should go. He couldn't take another risk with the railroads or roads going out of town or boats going down the river. It was at a point where odds on all those things were too big. Now that he was here in Philadelphia he had to stay here. It was a big enough place. What he had to do was find a section of the city where they wouldn't be likely to pick him up, where he could take his time and pull himself together.

He knew Philadelphia because very long ago he had put in a couple of years at the University of Pennsylvania and at that time he had been an impressionable boy who liked to roam around alone and pick up things. In those two years he had covered a lot of Philadelphia, and he found out it was a lot of cities inside of a city. Germantown was complete in itself, and so was Frankford. Across the Schuylkill there was West Philadelphia with its University. And because the city was divided so distinctly he was thinking now that what he had to do was get away from the center and cross a few boundaries. He wondered if there was a lot of crime in Germantown. If things hadn't changed there wouldn't be much police activity up there, because long ago when he was at the University he saw Germantown as a collection of dignity, just a bit smug and perhaps unconsciously snobbish against the historical background and the old colonial flavor. It might still be quiet and dignified up there. He wished he had cab fare. The dime for beer left him eighty-three cents, and he knew a cab to Germantown would cost much more.

"God Almighty," he said, because even with the overcoat it was so biting cold, and he smiled remembering that this was why he had left the University, because these Philadelphia winters were just too much for him. He remembered one day when it was as miserable as a day can possibly be, no rain or snow but a cold grey day with meanness written all over the sky and the streets, and he decided he didn't have to put up with that sort of weather, even though he liked the atmosphere of the University and the things he was learning there. So he packed his things and took a train, feeling the luxury of walking out on something he didn't care for. But now there was no walking out, there was only running away. There was a vast difference between walking out and running away.

He walked down the alley, then went up Tenth to Spring Garden. The Delaware wind came crashing down the wide street, hitting him hard, almost knocking him flat. He needed food and he needed rest, and he went over to a street lamp and leaned against the pole, wondering if he should take the chance of going into a restaurant. Then all at once there was a policeman standing in front of him.

"Plenty cold," the policeman said.

"What?" Hart said. He had his hands away from the pole of the street lamp and he was wondering if he should run north or west or try his luck across the street and down another alley.

The policeman clapped black leather mitts together and said, "I said it's plenty cold."

"This?" Hart said. "This is nothing. You've never been in northern Canada."

"This is cold enough for me," the policeman said.

"This is summer, compared to where I've been," Hart said. He knew he hadn't lost any of it. It was still good, the way it came out, the way it sounded, with just the right balance between conviction and nonchalance. As long as he could hold on to that way of pitching words, he was all right.

He left the policeman standing there, and he walked west on Spring Garden Street, deciding on Germantown.

He walked up Tulpehocken Street, watching the fronts of houses and hoping to see a room-for-rent sign. He went up two blocks without seeing such a sign, and then he was on Morton Street and he decided to turn there and try two or maybe three blocks east on Morton. He was very careful about it as he walked along Morton Street, watching the doors, the porch posts, the brick walls underneath the porch, any place where there would be a sign. He was finished with one block, starting on the second, when from somewhere back in the blackness he heard the crackling sound that had fire in it, and he started to run.

He knew how to run. For one thing he was built for it and for another he had been working at it for a long time. Without extending himself he was covering a lot of ground, and presently he decided to have a look back there. He turned and looked back and all he could see was the street and houses on both sides of the street and the empty pavements.

That was all. That was what had been chasing him. The emptiness.

He made a fist and walked up to a tree. He slammed his fist against the tree and pain shot through his knuckles. Not enough pain. He had to cure himself now, get this ended before it could really get started, because once it got started he would have much difficulty curing it and maybe he wouldn't be able to cure it at all. He had to hurt himself more than this, make himself realize that he couldn't continue this sort of thing. The pain made him close his eyes. He told himself even if he had to break his hand he had to cure himself now. He shaped the hurt hand into an ever harder fist and readied another blow at the tree.

He had the fist in motion but something got into the focus of his eyes aiming at the tree. The fist stopped a few inches away from the tree. Hart turned and looked down the street. It was quiet, it was still. But it was no longer empty, because something dark was on the pavement a block away.

Hart walked toward the dark thing, knowing this was all wrong. He should be going in the other direction. But he couldn't be a machine all the time. He had to follow the emotional impulse once in a while, and now the impulse was pure curiosity and he kept going forward until at last he was there where the dark form of a man was motionless on the pavement.

Bending down, Hart saw the vague sign of life, the battle to breathe. He got his hands on the man's shoulders. He tugged, and rolled the man over and he had a look at the man's face.

He was a young man and he had his eyes open and he looked at Hart and said, "Are you a doctor?"

"No," Hart said.

"All right, then," the man said, "take a walk." He closed his eyes and his throat contracted and then some blood came out of his mouth. He opened his eyes and when he saw Hart still there he seemed surprised. He said, "What are you hanging around for?"

"I'm trying to think of a way to help you."

"Do you have a car?" the man said.

"No."

"Do you live around here?"

"No."

"Jesus Christ," the man said, and some more blood came out of his mouth. He tried to roll over and his face tightened and he started to let out a scream, forced it back just as it began to shoot from his mouth. And instead the blood came again, and again he said, "Jesus Christ." Then he looked at Hart and he said, "Do you know anyone around here?"

"No," Hart said. "But maybe I can help you anyway. Do you want to roll over?"

"All right," the man said, "roll me over."

Hart did it more gently this time. The man was face down and Hart saw the small hole very black against the yellow camel hair. It was halfway down and maybe two inches to the left of the spine. The man was going to die in a minute or so.

"Where is it?" the man said.

Hart told him.

"Jesus Christ," the man said. "I'm done." His shoulders began to quiver. He seemed to be crying. Then he made the sounds of dying and he was trying to get words into it. Hart bent low, trying to catch it. And he heard, "—pocket—wallet—you might as well—they want it—I don't want them to have it—you might as well—oh Jesus Christ oh Lord in Heaven it hurts it hurts—go on, take the wallet and get out of here and if you know what's good for you don't go to the police don't tell anybody just take the wallet and take the money out and throw the wallet away, you better burn it, that's right, burn it—now take it—now—buy your wife a diamond ring—buy your poor old mother a house—buy yourself a car—"

Hart heard something coming down the street. He twisted his head and he saw two figures a little more than a block away, running toward his eyes. He started to go away, then he twisted again and he had his hand underneath the camel's hair coat, going into the back pocket of heavy tweed sports slacks, getting a hold on a wallet. As he took the wallet out, the man who owned the wallet shuddered and died, and then Hart was on his feet, sprinting down Morton Street.

Someone yelled, "Stop!"

"Sure," Hart said. "Right away."

The crackling noise came again. Then again and three more times. He felt a bullet rip some fabric from his bright green coat. He knew he had to get off Morton Street but he couldn't see any alley on this block and he knew a side street wouldn't be any good. He was going to chance it for another block, if he could last that long. If he didn't see any alley by then, he was going to throw the wallet in the air and let them see it, and maybe they would leave him alone.

He crossed the side street, making it in two big jumps, then he was on his way again, going down Morton Street as fast as he could go. He saw an alley sliding toward him and then a bullet went by and it couldn't have been more than an inch under the lobe of his left ear. As he entered the alley he heard a door opening somewhere, a scream, the door shutting, and he could imagine the housewife fainting dead away.

Running down the alley he put the wallet in a coat pocket. He made a few more yards, selected his garden, vaulted a wood fence four feet high, went flat going backwards and finally hiding behind a bush.

He heard them coming down the alley.

If there was a market, he would have sold his chances for one thin dime. There were two lamps in the alley, and one of them was tossing light toward this garden. They were taking their time about it, going over each garden and Hart could hear them talking it over as they went along. They weren't excited. They were very sure about it, just as he was. He wondered what they wanted most, him or the wallet. If it was him, it was because they thought the dying man had said something that they didn't want repeated. If it was the wallet, it was because the wallet contained something they wanted.

Hart estimated that he had about twenty seconds at the outside. He took the wallet out of his pocket, edged it toward where the light from the lamp was thickest. The wallet was goatskin, very soft, and it opened smoothly and Hart took out eleven bills. They were thousand-dollar bills.

A voice said, "He's got to be somewhere around."

Another voice said, "Talk to him. We'll save time that way."

"All right," the first voice said. Then it was louder and it was saying, "Come on out, mister. You won't get hurt."

Hart was digging a hole behind the bush. When he thought it was deep enough he inserted the eleven thousand dollars and then he quickly patted the soil on top. He rubbed his soil-stained hands on his trousers, put the wallet back in his pocket, and heard the first voice saying, "I'm telling you you won't get hurt if you come out now. We just want to talk to you, that's all."

"Okay," Hart said, and as he got up and came out from behind the bush he said, "You got the wrong man. I didn't kill him."

He saw the two men watching him from the other side of the fence. One of them, tall and young and wearing a skater's wool cap and shaker sweater, went over and opened the gate. The other man, silver hair showing under a soft-brim felt, had a revolver pointed at Hart.

"Come on out and let's have a look at you," the silver-haired man said.

Hart went out through the opened gate. The young man in the skater's cap came up to him and threw a fist at his face. He was under it and the skater without skates was wide open for a left hook. Hart thought of the revolver and kept his hands down and knew he was going to get hit on the skater's next try and there was nothing he could do but stand there and take it. The skater pushed him against the fence, setting him up for a right cross. He stood there and the fist came toward his face and he let his head go back as the fist came in. It was a slow punch, but there was a lot of force in it, and it hurt.

The skater smiled. He had a long, thick nose that came to a knob at the end. He had big teeth in a thin face. Both cheeks were mottled with the scars from a bad case of some skin disease. The skater was getting ready to hit Hart again.

Hart looked at the man with silver hair and said, "Revolver or no revolver, if he tags me again he gets a busted pelvis."

The skater smiled very wide and said, "Well, whaddya know—he's a kicker."

The man with silver hair looked at the skater and said, "Choke him—we've made enough noise with bullets."

"Sure," Hart said, "go ahead and choke me." He extended his head and lifted his chin obligingly. The skater put up two large hands and showed the fingers to Hart, then walked in to put the fingers around Hart's throat. Hart stood where he was, stood quietly until the fingers were fastened on his throat, and then he brought up his left leg and his knee caught the skater between the legs and the skater let out a tremendous screech and went backward. Hart went along with him, grabbed him and threw him at the man with silver hair. The skater screeched again, colliding with the man with silver hair, and Hart heard the gun go off. The skater and the man with silver hair were on the ground and the skater was making weird noises and the man with silver hair was trying to aim the gun.

Hart was undecided. If he ran now he would have his back turned to the gun, and he wasn't sure he would be able to run fast enough. And if he stood here he was going to get shot. The only thing he felt right now was a definite regret that he had selected Germantown.

Now the gun was aimed and the man with silver hair was getting to his feet. The skater was on the ground, squirming and moaning. Hart raised his arms and smiled foolishly.

The man with silver hair was saying, "You're too much trouble."

Hart said, "I don't know about you, but I don't like to be choked."

"Do you think I like to shoot people?"

"No," Hart said. "You're a nice guy. You're a swell guy. You wouldn't shoot anybody."

"Unless I had a reason."

"And would it have to be a good reason?"

"Sure," said the man with silver hair. "I don't like to shoot people. I don't get any special kick out of it."

"That's fine," Hart said. "That means you won't shoot me."

"That means I will shoot you."

"You think you've got a reason?"

"A good reason."

"Oh, all right," Hart said. "You want the wallet? I'll give you the wallet."

He took the wallet out of his pocket.

"Toss it," said the man with silver hair. "If it comes toward my eyes I'll shoot you in the stomach."

Hart tossed the wallet. The wallet was caught and pocketed. The man with silver hair was looking at Hart's face and saying, "We don't have too much time, Paul. See if you can stand up."

The skater was sobbing now. The skater said, "I'm ruptured. I'm all smashed down there."

"Take a look at it, Paul," said the man with silver hair.

"I'm afraid to look at it," the skater said.

"Go on, Paul. Look at it," said the man with silver hair.

Paul sobbed loudly. Paul said, "I'm afraid, Charley. I feel bad enough as it is. If I look at it I'll feel worse."

"What are we going to do?" Hart said. "Stand here?"

"I don't know," said the man with silver hair. "There's not much sense just standing here, is there?"

"I guess not," Hart said. He reasoned he could just about put two yardsticks between his chest and the revolver.

"It hurts something fierce," Paul said. "Charley, do something for me. I can't stand it."

Charley twisted his lips and bit at the inside of his mouth. He was thinking. He seemed to be looking past Hart's shoulder as he said, "Let's get him out of here."

They heard a police whistle. It was short, then it was long, then it was short twice. Then it was very long and then there were more whistles.

Charley bit hard at the inside of his mouth. "All right," he said, "let's get out of here fast. You take his legs. I'll have one hand on his wrist and one hand on the revolver. Turn your back to me and pick up his legs."

Hart obeyed. Paul groaned and was bringing it up to a yell when Charley said, "Now you cut that out, Paul."

Paul sobbed again. They were carrying him down the alley. He said, "I can't stand it, Charley. I just can't stand it, that's all."

"Let's hurry it up," Charley said.

Hart moved faster.

"Please, Charley—" Paul was groaning and sobbing. "Give me a break, will you?"

Charley had no reply for that. They were going rather fast down the alley. They heard the whistles again. As they came toward the end of the alley Charley said they ought to turn toward the right so they could get back to Tulpehocken. Paul was begging Charley to get him to a hospital. Hart was wondering if it would be a good idea to let go of Paul's legs and gamble on a sprint. Then they were at the end of the alley and turning into another alley.

"Let's hold it," Charley said. He was breathing heavily, taxed from supporting half of Paul's weight with one arm.

They listened for more whistles. They didn't hear anything.

"At least get me back to the house," Paul said.

"That's what we're trying to do," Charley said. "Do you think you can walk?"

Paul groaned.

"Give it a try," Charley said. "Let go of his legs, mister. Let's see if we can get him to stand."

Paul was groaning and telling them how bad it was as they got his feet on the ground and then lifted him upright. His knees gave way and they tried it again. On the fifth try they had him standing.

Charley said, "You're all right, Paul."

Paul looked at Hart and said, "I'll be talking with you later. You can think about that."

"Should I let it get me?" Hart asked.

Paul didn't answer. Charley gestured with the revolver and said, "You help him. I'll walk in back."

They walked slowly. Paul began to groan again. They

went down this second alley, crossed a narrow street and they were in another alley. Then still another and they came out on Morton. They started to walk up Morton and Charley changed his mind and said they better use the alley and the back entrance. They went back into the alley going parallel with Morton Street. As they walked up the alley, Hart was counting the houses. When they came to the seventh house, Charley said that was it. He told Hart to walk up the steps and knock five times on the back door.

Hart went up the steps and saw dim lights coming from the front of the house. He knocked five times. As he waited for a response he wondered if it would be a good idea to leap off the back porch and gamble on the darkness of the alley. He turned and looked at Charley and saw the high polish of the revolver.

The door opened. A fat woman with fluffy platinum blonde hair looked at Hart and was still looking at him when Charley said, "Come on down here, Frieda. I want you to give Paul a hand."

"What's the matter with Paul?" the fat woman wanted to know.

Hart was wondering what the chances were of grabbing the fat woman and getting her in front of him as a shield, then ducking in, closing the door, racing through the house and going out through the front door. He decided it wasn't a good idea. It was too complicated. He decided to hang around for a while. Maybe an easier opening would show itself.

Charley was up the steps now, telling him to enter the house. He heard the footsteps of Frieda and Paul, very careful and slow against the creaking wood. They were in the kitchen. Charley turned on the light. It was a small neat kitchen with an old-fashioned stove and an old-fashioned ice box. Footsteps came from the front of the house and Hart heard voices. He studied two men as they came into the kitchen. They were strongly built tall men and they wore dark worsted suits, well cut and smartly styled. One of them was good-looking.

They looked at Hart.

The good-looking one said, "What do you call this?"

"I call it aggravation," Charley said.

"*You* call it aggravation," Hart said.

"Look, Charley," the good-looking one said, "we don't need this."

"We won't need it later," Charley said. ''Right now we need it. We need it here."

"I could use a smoke," Hart said.

Frieda was helping Paul into another room. The black-haired man who was not good-looking took a pack of cigarettes out of a coat pocket, flipped the pack so that two cigarettes jumped out, extended the pack to Hart. The good-looking one struck a match.

Hart took smoke in and let it out. "Much obliged."

Then they ignored Hart. They faced Charley and the good-looking one said, "Well, we're already packed."

"You can unpack," Charley said. "We got Renner."

"Where?" the good-looking one asked.

"In the alley," Charley said. "I knew I hit him, but I didn't see him drop. When we got up there we couldn't see him. We went out on Morton Street and we didn't see him there either. Paul didn't like Morton Street and I was afraid too, so we went back into the alley and talked it over. Finally I said he had to be on Morton Street so we went out of the alley again and we tried the other side of Morton Street. Then we came back to this side and we saw this guy with him. This guy saw us and started to run. We ran after him and when we got up to Renner we stopped just long enough to see if he was finished."

"Was he finished?" the good-looking one said.

"Yes," Charley said. "He was all done, so we kept running after this guy and finally we got him in a back yard. Paul had to go and get tough so this guy gave Paul a knee."

The good-looking one turned and looked at Hart. "Where did you get connected with Renner?"

"I don't think he was connected with Renner," Charley said.

"Maybe he was," the good-looking one said.

"Listen to Charley," Hart said. "He's got the brains."

The good-looking one made a fist and showed it to Hart. "How long since you've been to a dentist?"

"I'm sure he wasn't connected with Renner," Charley said. "He was just curious. But I'll make sure anyway. As long as we got him here we don't need to worry about it."

"Did you get the case from Renner?"

"I got the case," Charley said. "I didn't get it from Renner. I got it from the guy."

"What do you mean you got it from the guy?"

"This guy took Renner's wallet."

The good-looking one turned to the one who wasn't good-looking and said, "Give me one of your cigarettes."

Hart took off his overcoat and arranged it neatly over a chair.

The good-looking one pointed a lighted cigarette at Charley and said, "You've got to face things, Charley. This guy was connected with Renner. The wallet proves it." He turned and placed a clean hand with manicured fingers on the shoulder of the other man. He said, "Maybe Rizzio here has an outside connection. How do we know?"

"That's a nice thing to say," said Rizzio.

"I'm not trying to hurt your feelings, Rizzio," said the one who was good-looking. "But here's a game where we've got to close every opening. Maybe I have an outside connection. Maybe Frieda. Maybe Myrna. Maybe even Charley. You see what I'm getting at? Who would have thought Renner would pull something like that? If we're going to get dividends out of this we can't let any openings stay open."

"There's a lot to that," Charley admitted. "I'll take one of your cigarettes, Rizzio."

Hart walked around them, took one of the chairs, sighed as he relaxed in it. He leaned an elbow on the table and sat there watching them.

Charley showed him the revolver to remind him it was still around. Then Charley turned to Rizzio and said, "Where's the car?"

"Where I parked it," Rizzio said.

"Go upstairs," Charley said.

"What's upstairs?" Rizzio said.

"Take a look at Paul," Charley said. "Then come down and tell me what condition he's in."

Rizzio walked out of the kitchen.

Charley and the good-looking one stood there smoking and looking at each other. After some moments they both turned and looked at Hart. Then they looked at each other again.

"What do we do with this guy?" the good-looking one said.

"We talk to him," Charley said.

"I'll talk to him," the good-looking one said.

"Don't get tough with him, Mattone," Charley said.

"Why not?"

"If you get tough with him he'll hit back."

The good-looking one started to rub a fist, grinning at Hart and saying, "I like that. I like when they hit back."

"If he hits back you'll lose your temper and kill him," Charley said. "I want him alive for a while. Maybe he's got some talent we can use."

"Are you trying to sell me something?" Hart said.

"Let me hit him once," Mattone said. "Just to give him the idea."

Charley worked the cigarette for a lot of smoke, got it out slowly at first, then steamed it out in a sudden volley. "Look, Mattone, I said I didn't want you to hit him."

Charley started to walk out of the kitchen. Mattone touched his arm and said, "What about cops?"

"There were cops."

"They see you?"

"We heard whistles."

"They'll be dragging the neighborhood," Mattone said. "As long as we're packed already—"

"No," Charley said. "We stay where we are."

"Wait a minute, Charley—"

"I said we're going to stay right where we are," Charley said. He walked out of the kitchen.

Mattone reached into his jacket pocket and took out a revolver. He grinned at Hart and then he walked toward the vacant chair. The grin widened as he saw the bright green coat hanging over the back of the chair. Then he looked at Hart and he looked at the chocolate-brown flannel suit and he came over and rubbed a finger on the fine quality flannel. He walked back to the other chair and put a hand against the bright green Lapama fleece. He looked at Hart again and he said, "It doesn't figure."

"Every man has his ups and downs," Hart said.

Mattone raised the front of the coat and had a look inside the label. He looked at Hart and he said, "You mean to tell me you went into that place and bought a coat?"

"I went into that place and stole a coat," Hart said.

"Oh." Mattone took the cigarette out of his mouth, held it delicately as he sat down at the table across from Hart. "You stole the coat. What else did you steal?"

"Nothing."

"Nothing from that place. How about other places?"

"Nothing."

"You see?" Mattone said. "We're starting all wrong. You stole the wallet, didn't you?"

"No," Hart said. "I didn't steal the wallet. He told me to take it."

Mattone leaned forward. "Take a good look at me."

Hart took the look. He said, "No, you don't look like a moron. And I'm not talking to you as if you were a moron. That's what happened. He told me to take the wallet."

"Why would he want you to have the wallet?"

"Ask him."

Mattone turned and crossed one leg over the other and put cigarette ashes on the floor. He grinned at the ashes. He said, "You're going to be a pleasure. A real pleasure. I've been away from the ring a long time. You know how it is. I get so I want to put my fists on a face. How much do you weigh?"

"One forty."

Mattone let out a brief laugh. He looked at the revolver in his hand. He said, "I guess I won't need this."

He put the revolver in his jacket pocket.

"Do you use rouge?" Hart said.

"What's the matter, are you in a hurry for it?"

"The eyebrows," Hart said. "Do you pluck them every day?"

"Three times a week," Mattone said. "You're going to get it now. You can't take it back."

"Oh, come on," Hart said. "You're not that angry. You're not angry at all. You just want some fun. But remember what Charley said."

"Now that's funny," Mattone said as he stood up. "I can't remember. That's my big weakness. My memory."

"You're a scream," Hart said.

Mattone's eyes were bright with joy. "This is wonderful. He's begging for it."

"Can't live without it."

"All right, stand up and get it."

Hart stood up and sat down quickly to get away from a straight right aimed at the mouth. Mattone leaned over to try the right again and Hart brought up a shoe and kicked Mattone a few inches below the kneecap. Mattone hopped back and lowered a hand toward the knee and Hart stood up and leaned on the right side and then brought up a right hand uppercut and missed. Mattone went hopping back and started to dance. Hart started to go forward, then stepped back quickly, reached down and grabbed a chair leg. As Mattone came in to break up the chair project, Hart already had the chair in both hands and he threw it at Mattone's face. Mattone stopped the chair with his arms, stumbled over it as he rushed at Hart, and Hart's face was all twisted with effort, body and arms working fast, fists hitting Mattone in the nose, in the lips, on the chin. Mattone was bleeding and he wasn't liking it. He hit Hart in the chest, hit him again in the ribs, had him against the wall, showed him a right hand and hit him with the right hand three times on the jaw. Hart started to go down and his head was hanging low and he saw Mattone dropping the right hand and getting it ready for the uppercut. Hart let his head go down still further until it was down against Mattone's stomach. Then Hart brought his head up as fast as he could and the top of his skull caught Mattone under the chin.

"Oh," Mattone said, and then he was unconscious. Hart grabbed him under the armpits as he started to go down. Then Hart lowered him slowly and when he was on the floor Hart bent over him and reached for the shoulder holster.

"No," Charley said. "Don't do that."

Charley was in the doorway and he had his revolver with him.

"I wish I could get a decent break," Hart said. He straightened up with his arms hanging loosely at his sides.

"You got no kick coming," Charley said. "You're getting all the breaks. If you'd made it with his gun you'd be on your way out the back door and I'd be shooting at you from the living room. You're drawing all good cards tonight."

"Sure. I'm so happy I feel like singing. Did you see any of it?"

"I came in when he was ready to give you the uppercut. I had an idea you were going to give him your head under the chin. I was going to warn him about that, but you were handling it pretty and I wanted to see if you'd get away with it."

Hart put a hand to his jaw. His jaw wasn't swollen, but it hurt.

"What started it?" Charley asked.

"I wanted to know if he used rouge."

Charley went over, picked up the overturned chair. He brought up a knee, rested a foot on the chair, leaned his arms on his leg, keeping the revolver aimed at Hart. He said, "You continue this sort of thing and I'm going to tie you up."

"Suppose I don't continue this sort of thing?"

Charley appreciated that. He nodded. He said, "That was all right. That was a peach. You got me there."

"Sure, I got you. Like a monkey in the cage has the keeper outside." And then he said, "What time is it?"

Charley glanced at a wristwatch. "Eight-twenty."

"I had breakfast at seven this morning. Nothing since then."

"What stopped you?"

"Broke."

"All right," Charley said. "We'll fix you up. What's your name?"

"Al."

"All right, Al. I'll have Frieda arrange a meal for you. All you need to do now is start something with Frieda."

Rizzio walked into the kitchen and looked at Mattone and said, "What happened to him?"

"He saw a mouse," Hart said.

Charley looked at Rizzio and said, "Go get Frieda."

Rizzio started out of the kitchen and Charley said, "Hold it. How is Paul?"

Rizzio said, "He's causing a lot of commotion up there, but he's all right."

"Give me a cigarette," Charley said.

Rizzio took the pack out of his pocket and looked at Hart and said, "That's all I do around here. I run up and down steps and I drive the car and I supply everybody with cigarettes."

Rizzio held a match to Charley's cigarette and said, "I'll get Frieda." He left the kitchen.

Charley went over to the sink and loaded a glass with cold water. He went over to Mattone and threw the water on Mattone's face.

Mattone sat up and looked at Charley. Then he looked at Hart. Then he stood up and rubbed wetness from his face. He took a large white handkerchief from the top pocket of his worsted suit and pressed the handkerchief against his face. Then he walked past Charley and went out of the kitchen.

"A fine boy," Hart said.

"At one time he was a smart light heavy," Charley said. "Then one night he came up against a body puncher and he went to the hospital with kidney trouble. When he came out of the hospital he started to gain weight. He became a heavy and one night a colored boy hit him high up on the jaw and gave him a concussion. When he came out of the hospital he got connected with a mob in South Philly and started to pick up numbers. One night he was in a pool-room and he saw a guy he didn't like making a call in the phone booth. He picked up a billiard ball and slung it clear across the room and it went into the phone booth. The guy came out of the phone booth with a fractured skull. Mattone did a year for that. He was on his way to gasoline station and grocery store jobs and I met him one night and told him he could do better. He told me to leave him alone. One night he was robbing a gasoline station and the attendant hit him in the kidney with a monkey wrench. He got away but he was in the hospital for the better part of a month. When he came out he looked me up. He's been with me ever since."

"How long ago was that?" Hart asked.

"Two years ago."

Frieda came into the kitchen.

Charley said, "Fix him a meal. I'm going into the living

room." He looked at Hart. "Frieda could go to Iowa and be a champion hog caller. I'll have the revolver in my lap. Put it together."

"It's together," Hart said.

Charley left the kitchen.

Frieda was a big woman. She was one-sixty if she was an ounce, more solid than soft, packed into five feet five inches and molded majestically. He guessed she didn't wear a girdle and when she turned her back to him and leaned over slightly he was certain of it. She was wearing another dress now, a purple creation that was more than just tight. It looked as if it had grown up with her. He remembered before she had been wearing a plain house dress and he wondered if the purple dress was for his bene-fit. She bent over even further. Her calves were the same as the rest of her, solid round fat coming down rhythmically to slim ankles giving way to high-heeled shoes that she hadn't been wearing before.

She turned around and looked at him. She said, "You like eggs?"

"Scrambled."

"You like scrapple?"

"Like poison."

"I'll make you something nice. You like coffee?"

"I live on it."

She smiled. She wanted him to examine her and he examined her. The platinum blonde hair fluffed all over her head and rolled on her forehead and came down behind her ears to a big fluff at the back. Her eyes were brown, clear and healthy. Very little mascara. And underneath her smoothly shaped nose her large mouth was deep red with some purple in the red paint. The rouge on her pink round face was deeper pink with a trace of·purple in it.

There wasn't a line on her face.

Hart frowned with interest and said, "You keep yourself in good condition."

"I manage." Her voice was full and solid.

"I'm trying to guess your age," Hart said.

"Thirty-four. I've been married four times."

"You married now?"

"I guess so. I don't know what he's doing. I don't know where he is. The last time I heard it was Cincinnati. That was a year ago. Really interesting boy, and generous, too, but he played too rough."

"What did you do to him?"

"I broke his collarbone with a silver hand-mirror he gave me for my birthday."

"Did that do it?"

"No. He wanted more. When he got out of the hospital he traced me to Florida. I had to spit in his face a few times and the last time it was in front of a lot of people. And that was what did it. He hauled off on me but I was with a professional wrestler that night. He really tried with that wrestler. He lasted almost five minutes, then he went flying over a few tables and they had to carry him out. I didn't see him after that until he looked me up in Cincinnati. He wanted money. That tickled me. I got such a kick out of it that I actually gave him money."

Hart shaped a laugh and let her hear it. She laughed with him.

Then she waited on him. She was a good cook, and she knew the finer details, all on the modern side. She sat there watching him enjoying it.

He was slow with the second cup of coffee. He had his eyes on the blackness in the cup, knowing she had her eyes on him. He knew he had started a wedge but he didn't want to widen it too quickly because then it might break.

He said, "Did you hear about Renner?"

"Yes," she said. "Paul told me."

"How is Paul?"

"I gave him a couple pills. I guess he's sleeping now. He'll be all right. If you're still around when he's on his feet you're in for a terrible lacing."

"I don't think I'll be around. Is that real platinum blonde?"

"No, and you know it isn't. You don't think you'll get away, do you?"

"Yes, Frieda," he said solemnly. "I can't help it, but that's what I think."

"Suppose you get away," she said, as if she didn't hear his last remark. "What would you do then?"

"I'd stay away."

"Would you open your mouth?"

"If I was a fool."

"That sounds like something. Build on it."

He said, "I'm wanted in New Orleans."

"For what?"

"Murder."

She leaned her head to one side and smiled dimly. "Now look," she said, "you're not trying to show me a good time, are you?"

"You wanted me to build. So I'm building."

"All right, build some more. Who was it?"

"My older brother."

"What name you using?"

"Al."

"Look, Al, you mean to sit there and tell me you killed your own brother?"

"Sure."

Frieda stood up. "Charley!"

Footsteps came banging toward the kitchen. Charley appeared in the doorway with the revolver all ready. Charley said, "What's he doing?"

Frieda said, "Charley, I want you to hear something." She looked at Hart. "Go ahead, tell it to Charley."

Hart drained the cup and said, "I'm telling him because you're asking me to. I told you because you asked me. Just remember that." He turned his head toward Charley. "I told her I'm wanted in New Orleans for killing my brother."

Charley rested the revolver flat in one palm and smoothed the other palm over it. Then Charley said, "Why did you skip?"

"I had no alibi," Hart said.

Frieda said, "Why did you pick Philadelphia?"

"I couldn't get a boat across the Gulf," Hart said. "I couldn't go north at first because I couldn't get the right connections. I had to go east. I went to Birmingham and from there I went north. This is as far as I got."

"When did you come in? How?" Charley's voice was quiet.

"The afternoon train from Baltimore," Hart said. "Some men in plain clothes stepped on the train when we pulled in at Thirtieth Street Station. I didn't know what they wanted and I wasn't going to stay there to find out. I got out of my seat and took a walk into the next car. Some more men in plain clothes were watching the doors. I kept walking through the cars. I was about two cars from the end and I had to turn around and look. So I turned around and I saw two of them coming after me. The next door was unguarded and I took that door before any of them could come down there from the outside. I had to leave all my belongings on the train, and that included about seven hundred dollars tucked away in a Gladstone."

"I think you got a weakness there," Charley said. "What's wrong with a wallet?"

"When you're running away you do funny things."

"It's still weak," Charley said.

"All right, it's weak," Hart said. "Tonight I walked into a store on Broad Street and stole the overcoat you see there on the chair."

Charley looked at the overcoat. "Broad and where?"

"Above Callohill."

"All right," Charley said. "What store?"

"I think it said Sam and Harry."

Frieda was looking at the bright green overcoat. She said, "It looks brand new."

Charley turned to Frieda. Charley said, "Get the telephone book and look up Sam and Harry in the classified section under men's clothing. Come in and tell me if there's a Sam and Harry clothing store on Broad Street above Callohill. And bring Mattone in with you."

Frieda walked out.

Charley put a forefinger through the trigger guard and twirled the revolver. "You don't mind a little checking, do you?"

Hart shook his head. He looked at the floor. Charley leaned against the icebox and kept twirling the revolver.

They could hear the flipping of telephone-book pages from the living room. Then Frieda came walking into the kitchen and Mattone was behind her.

Frieda said, "There's a Sam and Harry on Callohill Street above Broad."

Charley acted as if he didn't hear. Charley said to Mattone, "Take a look at that overcoat."

Mattone went over and examined the overcoat. He rubbed the bright green fabric between his fingers.

"Would you say that was quality?" Charley said.

Mattone said, "If I know anything about clothing it's a ninety-dollar article and it doesn't come from Sam and Harry."

Charley looked at Hart, and Hart looked at Mattone and said, "You're some brain, you are. Ten minutes ago you were looking at the Sam and Harry label."

Mattone dropped the coat and went over to Hart and took a swing and connected. Hart walked backward to the stove, came away from the stove and put his arms down to break the fall. Then he was on his knees and after that he was face down on the floor.

Charley said, "Stay with him, Frieda."

"Let me stay with him," Mattone said.

Charley looked at Mattone. "You come with me."

They went into the living room. Charley picked up the telephone book, found the number and made the call. When he got his party he said, "Did someone steal an overcoat from your place tonight?"

At the other end a voice said, "Just a minute—"

Charley hung up. He looked at Mattone. He said, "They want to trace the call. Is that good enough for you?"

"Look, Charley, I don't like that guy."

"And I don't like you," Charley said. "But I put up with you because you know your work. I like the way you work, but there's got to be satisfaction on both sides. Do you like the pay?"

"Look, Charley—"

"Do you like the pay?"

"I like the pay."

"All right, then, do as you're told. And don't do things I don't want you to do."

In the kitchen Hart was sitting up and tapping fingers against his jaw. Frieda was sitting at the table, leaning her face on a cupped hand and watching Hart and then turning as Charley came in. She looked at Charley's eyes.

Hart stood up and said, "Did you make the call?"

"Yes," Charley said. "If you want to go now you can go."

"What would you advise me to do?" Hart asked.

"Go back to New Orleans," Charley said. "You're already traced here, I mean as far as Philly, because of that Gladstone—that is, if you bought the Gladstone down south."

"I bought the Gladstone in Nashville after I threw away the other bag. But I was traced to Nashville."

"That means you're traced here, so your best move is to go back and do your hiding in New Orleans. Don't try little towns. Little towns are bad."

"I'm broke," Hart said.

Charley put a hand in a trousers pocket and took out some bills. He handed Hart a ten-dollar bill.

"Much obliged," Hart said. He pocketed the bill and put on his overcoat. He looked at the kitchen doorway. Then he looked at the back door.

Charley said, "Stay away from Tulpehocken until you get to Germantown Avenue. Then come back to Tulpehocken and get your trolley. If I were you I'd go to Frankford tonight and stay there a few weeks and try to pick up a little change. Then I'd go straight back to New Orleans and put it on a speculation basis for at least a month. Then I'd try the Gulf or I'd try the border from Texas."

Hart opened the back door and walked out. The cold air slammed into him like a sheet of stiff iced canvas. He went down the alley, and every few seconds he would turn around and look and listen carefully. Finally he decided that Charley probably wasn't following him after all. Hart knew what Charley would do instead. Charley was smart. Charley would know where to wait for Hart—and the eleven thousand. Hart figured Charley would give him another five minutes, at the outside, before he took off to do what he would have to do when Hart didn't show up. It was cold, and Hart was no fool. He'd show, all right.

Some thirty yards down the alley he came to his garden and began digging away at the cold hard soil.

He rolled up the eleven thousand dollars, inserting the bills into an overcoat pocket. Then he walked along the alley and headed back to the house.

The door opened and Charley stood there, showing Hart the revolver.

"All right," Charley said. "Come on in."

Hart entered the kitchen. He saw Frieda sitting at the table and looking up from a movie magazine. He took the rolled bills from the overcoat pocket and extended the money to Charley.

Charley took the bills and counted them.

"All there?" Hart said.

"All there," Charley said.

Frieda frowned. "What goes on here?"

Charley smiled mildly. "Al brought back the money."

Frieda pointed to the bills in Charley's hand. "That's the money Renner took."

Charley widened the smile. He said, "Frieda, you're right in there."

Hart said, "You knew there was nothing in the wallet. So all you did was send me out for the money."

Charley nodded slowly.

Hart said, "You were giving me around five minutes to get back here with the money, and if I wasn't back by then you were going to go out and wait at Germantown and Tulpehocken and get me there."

"Is that why you came back?"

"Not exactly," Hart said.

"All right," Charley said. "Let's have it complete. Why did you come back?"

"It's too cold out there."

"You mean it's too hot out there."

Hart grinned. "It's both. I don't need this weather. And I don't need all that Law running after me. Only thing I need is a place to hide. Only place I can hide is here."

"I thought you'd see it that way," Charley said.

They stood there grinning at each other. And then Charley said, "You owe me ten dollars."

Hart took out the ten and handed it to him. "That's for a week's room and board."

"You're getting a bargain," Charley said. He went to the

doorway and called for Rizzio. He told Rizzio there was a folding-cot somewhere in the cellar and he wanted it brought upstairs. Without looking at Hart, he murmured, "I hope you'll be comfortable."

Frieda got up from the table and moved toward the sink. As she passed Hart, her hand drifted down and she touched him. She said, "I think he'll be comfortable."

They could hear Rizzio banging around in the cellar and then they could hear him battling with the cot up to the second floor. Mattone entered the kitchen and helped himself to a glass of milk and some chocolate cookies. Frieda was with the movie stars again and eating an apple. Hart leaned against the back door and looked at the floor. Charley was standing in the middle of the kitchen and biting the inside of his mouth and looking at nothing. The kitchen was quiet except for the sound of energetic munching as Frieda ate the apple.

Someone was coming down from the second floor, coming through the house. She came into the kitchen, an extremely thin girl about five-two with extremely white skin and very black hair. Hart didn't have time to note the color of her eyes because just then Charley turned toward the door and told Hart to follow him.

They went through the house. It was just another quiet little row house in quiet Germantown. The cleanliness of the kitchen was extended through the rest of the house.

In the room where Rizzio put the cot, Hart saw two watercolors hanging on the wall; both were signed "Rizzio."

"They're very good," Hart said.

"Are you telling me they're good?" Rizzio said.

"Hurry up with that cot and get out of here," Charley said.

"I can't find anything wrong with them," Hart said.

Rizzio took hold of Charley's arm and said, "You hear that?"

"All right," Charley said, "one of these days I'll sponsor

an exhibition. If you're finished with that cot, take a walk. Give me two cigarettes before you go," he added.

Rizzio obeyed and faced the wall and stared unhappily at his water-colors. Then he walked out of the room and closed the door. Charley handed a cigarette to Hart and then took a match out of his pocket and struck it on the sole of his shoe.

Charley seated himself on the edge of the wide bed and Hart sat on the edge of the cot.

Charley said, "You'll share this room with me and Rizzio."

Hart gazed contentedly at the window beside the cot. He said, "I'm first in line for the fresh air."

Charley smiled and said, "A crook tried to climb through that window a month ago. Rizzio hit him in the face and threw him out the window. We went down and picked him up out of the back yard, the alley part along this side of the house. He had a broken back and both legs were broken. Mattone ended it for him with a knife and then we put him in the car and rode to a quiet street and threw him in the gutter."

"Where did Renner sleep?" Hart said.

"Don't ask questions about Renner. Don't ask questions about anything. If I feel like telling you, I'll tell you. Renner slept in the back room with Paul and Mattone. There's three beds in the back room but I don't want you in there with Paul and Mattone. You wouldn't last long with them. I want you to stay away from them as much as you can—until they get used to you. And now here's what we do. We take mansions on the Main Line. Every section where there's wealth. I think there's more wealth concentrated in the Philly Main Line than any city in the country. We don't load ourselves down. We take just enough to make a profitable little haul. Two or three burlap bags, never more than that, and it's mostly silverware and antiques. We got a fence connection in South Philly and he's been working with me for seventeen years, and we have a fairly good arrangement. What brought out that comment about Rizzio's water-colors?"

"They're good," Hart said.

"How do you know they're good?"

"It's just one man's opinion, but I know a little about it. I majored in fine arts at Pennsylvania."

"Do you do any painting yourself?"

"No, but I've done a lot of collecting. In New Orleans I had a very nice collection."

"What else did you do in New Orleans?"

"I loafed. I could afford to. My old man piled up about three million in beet sugar. He left it to my mother and when she died she left it to my older brother Haskell."

"Is that why you killed him?"

"Yes," Hart said. "I wanted the money."

"How many brothers altogether?"

"Three of us. Haskell, myself and Clement."

"Any sisters?"

"Two of them and they're both dead. They were students at Tulane and one night they were coming home from a dance and the car turned over a few times. I belong to a very happy family."

Charley was looking at Rizzio's water-colors. Charley said, "Was this Haskell married?"

"No."

"Clement?"

"Clement married when he was eighteen. Now they've got three children and it's one of those unusual marriages. I mean it's really a pleasant arrangement."

Charley leaned back on his elbows, the cigarette tight in his mouth and snapping up and down as he said, "Let's hear something about the killing."

"Well," Hart said, "I did it with a blackjack. I wanted to make it look like burglary. Haskell lived alone in a big home near Audubon Park. I went up there one night and got in through the back door without any of the servants seeing me. And I know they didn't see me get into his room. I hit him over the head with the blackjack and kept on hitting him until he was dead. Then I went through his room and took all his jewelry—he went in for diamond-studded watches and emerald cuff links and that sort of thing. He had fifteen hundred dollars in his wallet. I thought it was going to look like a genuine burglary, because I got away all right, and the room was messed up and so forth. But later I was worried. The police were putting too many things together. Besides, they had a witness who saw me near Audubon Park that night, and it knocked my alibi to bits. When I saw they were really closing in on me I took a walk."

Charley stood up, walked around the bed and placed himself in front of Rizzio's water-colors. Frowning at the paintings, he said, "I'm not sure, Al. Maybe we can use you right in on the jobs or maybe it would be better for you to go with Myrna and Frieda to get the leads. But I don't know about this painting business. I've always found it best to stay away from oils and that sort of thing. And the fence will have something to say about it. So we'll just let it ride for awhile, even though I've got the feeling your knowledge would come in handy."

"What do I do meanwhile?"

"Just stay here. I'll find things for you to do. You don't get bored easily, do you?"

"Not easily."

"You want to go to sleep now or do you want to come down and listen to the radio for awhile?"

"I think I'll go to sleep."

"All right, Al. I'll see you in the morning." Charley glanced again at Rizzio's paintings and then he walked out.

In the middle of an endless plain of soft snow there was a pool of black water. A man's head emerged from the pool and the man opened his mouth and began to shriek.

Hart opened his eyes and sat up. There was movement on the other side of the room, then the lights went on. Charley was there with his hand still near the light switch and Rizzio was getting out of bed. The shrieking came from the back room.

Mattone came rushing into the middle room and said, "Listen, that boy needs a doctor."

Charley followed Mattone out of the room. Rizzio inserted his feet into slippers and went out after them. Then Hart heard Charley saying, "You go back to bed," and a few moments later Rizzio re-entered the room and closed the door.

"Open the door," Hart said. "I want to hear what's going on."

Rizzio opened the door. They could hear the shrieking

from the back room. They could hear Frieda's voice and Charley's voice. Rizzio produced an unopened pack of cigarettes out of nowhere, along with a book of matches.

"You want one of these?" Rizzio said.

The shrieking became higher and louder.

"Let's have one," Hart said.

Rizzio came over and gave him a cigarette and a light. They listened to the shrieking from the front room. All at once the shrieking stopped and the talking went down to a murmur and then the murmur stopped. Hart had the cigarette in his mouth as he sat there rigid on the cot, watching the quiet wall beyond the opened door. A shadow hit the wall and Charley followed the shadow and entered the room.

Charley said, "Paul passed away."

"No," Rizzio said.

"All right, no," Charley said. He was looking at Hart. He said, "I didn't think it was that bad, even though I knew it was bad enough. You must have broken him to bits in there. He had internal bleeding and I guess the blood went up and choked his heart, or something. I don't know."

"Why didn't we get a doctor?" Rizzio said.

Charley looked at Rizzio and said, "I'll let you answer that."

"We ought to have our own doctor," Rizzio said.

Charley looked at Hart. "We used to have our own doctor. He died a few months ago. I've been looking around, but there's a shortage of doctors nowadays, especially the kind of doctors we need. It's a problem."

Rizzio was rubbing his chin and saying, "What are we going to do with Paul?"

"That's another problem," Charley said. "Is the furnace hot?"

"Jesus Christ, Charley."

"When I ask you a question," Charley said, "why don't you give me a direct answer?"

"I guess it's hot," Rizzio said. "I put in some coal a couple hours ago."

"Do we have a meat cleaver downstairs?" Charley asked.

"Oh Jesus Christ, Charley, I don't know, I don't know."

Charley turned and looked at Hart and said, "I got some

organization here." Then he turned again to Rizzio and said, "Come on, we'll take Paul downstairs."

"Wait just a minute, Charley, please." Rizzio was putting fingers in a bathrobe pocket. "Let me smoke a cigarette first."

"Smoke the cigarette later. It'll taste better then," Charley said.

Rizzio said, "What are you going to do, cut him up?"

"No," Charley said. "I'm going to put him in starch and shrink him. Do you want to help me carry him down or do you want to stand there and smoke cigarettes?"

"Charley, listen—"

"No, I don't have time to listen." Charley went back to the window sill. He was biting the inside of his mouth.

Hart sat very still. He could feel it coming and he was afraid of it but there was nothing he could do about it.

Charley looked at Hart and said, "Mattone's no good for it, either. Mattone's only good for causing a commotion. And I can't carry him down by myself."

"All right," Hart said. He got out of bed. Charley came off the window sill and looked at the pajamas and grinned.

"My best silk pajamas," Charley said.

They were pale green pajamas, and Hart was thinking dizzily of pale green background and dark bright red.

They went into the back room. Paul was naked on the bed and his eyes were half-closed and didn't seem like part of his face.

"Take his legs," Charley said.

They carried Paul downstairs. Hart was shivering. He was telling himself it was because the house was cold. They carried Paul down the cellar steps. They had Paul in the cellar and they put him on the floor near the furnace. Charley told Hart to stay with Paul, then Charley went upstairs and he was up there for a full five minutes, and Hart heard clanking around, as if Charley was looking for something. Then Charley came down the steps and in one hand he had a hack-saw and in the other hand he had a large knife.

Charley said, "Get some newspapers."

The front of the cellar was divided into two sections, one for coal, the other for old things that didn't matter too much. There was a pile of newspapers. Hart lifted half the pile and carried it toward the furnace.

"Get out of the way," Charley said. "I'm going to take his head off."

Hart stepped away, then went walking away as he heard the swish, the crunch, the grinding, the resistance, more grinding, the heavy breathing of Charley. Then the rustle of paper, the sound of paper getting wrapped around something. Then the furnace door opening. The sound of paper around something going into the fire. Then the furnace door closing.

"All right," Charley said. "I'll need you now."

Hart turned and came walking back. The light from a single bulb hanging from a long cord gave the cellar pure white light getting grey as it came toward the furnace. Under the grey light the headless body of Paul was grey-purple. Hart wondered if he could go through with this.

"Hold the legs tight," Charley said. "Hold them tight."

Hart took hold of the legs and closed his eyes. The sounds of the hack-saw and the knife were great big bunches of dreadful gooey stuff hitting him and going into him and he was getting sick and he tried to get his mind on something else, and he came to painting and started to concentrate on the landscapes of Corot, then got away from Corot although remaining in the same period as he thought of Courbet, then knowing Courbet was an exponent of realism and trying to get away from Courbet, unable to get away because he was thinking of the way Gustave Courbet showed Cato tearing out his own entrails and showed "Quarry," in which the stag under the tree was getting torn to bits by yowling hounds, and he tried to come back to Corot, past Corot to the gentle English school of laced garments and graceful posture and the delicacy and all that, and Courbet dragged him back.

And Charley said, "Hold him higher up."

With his eyes shut tightly, Hart said, "Tell me, Charley, did you ever do this before?"

"No," Charley said.

Hart opened his eyes and he saw the blood and he closed his eyes again. Charley was telling him to do things and he had to open his eyes to keep at it, but it was as if his eyes were closed, because he was gazing past the activity, and he was listening past the sounds of steel and flesh and paper. Now the work was going faster, the furnace door was opening and shutting in speedier rhythm, and yet time was bouncing all around the cellar, going so fast and melting as it went, so that finally time was all melted and there was no measuring it, and no measuring the smell of blood.

Then there was nothing on the floor but blood and newspapers. Charley went to the rear of the cellar, came back with a can of household cleanser. He ripped off the top of the can, threw the cleanser on top of the blood. Then he went away and came back with a bucket of hot water and a mop, and went to work. Hart took the unused newspapers back to the front of the cellar. Charley cleaned the tools, drying them as he came back.

They stood before the furnace and listened to the sound of burning.

"We better take these off," Charley said.

Hart looked at Charley, wondering what he meant, and saw that he meant the pajamas. And Hart looked at Charley's pajamas, looked at the blood all over pale blue, then he looked at the pajamas he was wearing, and he saw the pale green background and the gashes of dark bright red.

Charley opened the furnace door, threw in the pale blue pajamas, then Hart stepped over in front of the door and as he threw in the pale green pajamas he caught sight of the paper packages burning in there with a glaring purple and white flame. Then he caught a whiff of the smoke and he shut the door quickly.

"All right," Charley said, "let's go up."

They went upstairs. Coming away from the heat of the furnace area their naked bodies came into a cold living room and a colder stairway, and they moved quickly. They went into the bathroom and although there was no blood on their hands they washed their hands anyway.

Finally Hart climbed back into the cot, propped the pillows to make himself comfortable, sucked smoke into his mouth, filled himself up with the smoke and let it seep out between his teeth. He wondered why he wasn't sick. He thought maybe he was beginning to get tough. He told himself it didn't really make any difference, because he didn't give a hang, but underneath he knew he did give a hang and it made a lot of difference and no matter what he kept telling himself he was really afraid of what was happening inside him.

Hart settled back against the pillow and brought up his arms, resting flat on his back and folding his hands behind his head. Across the room he saw the glow of a lighted cigarette and he knew it came from Charley and he tried to think of what was in Charley's mind right now. Then he closed his eyes and he tried to sleep.

He worked on it for an hour. He was going toward sleep, trying to dive into it, pulled back by something and then he tried to crawl toward it, pulled back by the same something that was mostly memory and hardly any planning. He was beginning to feel tired and he made one big try, throwing everything out of his mind except one big circle on which he tried to ride as it went around in the blackness under his eyelids. He managed to get on the circle and it took him around a few times and then threw him off with violence. He opened his eyes and sat up and he could hear the steady breathing of Charley and the heavy, distorted breathing of Rizzio. He wondered where Rizzio kept the cigarettes.

He left the cot, moved quietly across the room and pulled on the chocolate flannel trousers over the fresh pajamas. Then as he worked himself into the chocolate flannel jacket he was facing the window and he could see the black out there without any lights in it. He put on socks and started to put on shoes and changed his mind. Then he was going out of the room and closing the door delicately. Then he was going down the dark hall, so dark that at first he had to guide himself by the wall, then getting lighter because of a thin and vague glow that came from downstairs. And it was confusing, because he remembered Charley putting out all lights downstairs before they came upstairs.

He was going down the stairway. The light remained vague, and it wasn't doing much against the darkness, but he was coming closer to it and for a moment he had the unaccountable feeling that the light had drawn him out of the cot and out of the room. Halfway down the stairway he knew that he could see the source of the light if he turned his head, and he didn't know why he didn't want to turn his head. But he had to turn his head when he reached the foot of the stairs, and when he did he saw the light coming from a small lamp with a blue velvety shade, dark blue to give the light that odd vagueness. The lamp was on a small table and next to the table someone was sitting in a high-backed chair. The entire arrangement, lamp and pale blue light and figure in white and the brown top of the chair, topping the white, amounted to a face, and it was the face of his dead brother, Haskell.

Hart wondered if he would cut himself to ribbons if he went headfirst through one of the front windows.

From the chair a feminine voice said, "Who is that?"

Hart took in what felt like a quart of air and let it out with his mouth wide open. He said, "It's Al."

"This is Myrna."

Her voice wasn't a whisper. It was lower than a whisper.

Hart said, "What bothers you?"

She said, "Paul was my brother."

The space between them was a block of quiet freezing with immeasurable speed.

It was that way for more than a minute, then she said, "What brought you downstairs?"

"I don't know. I couldn't sleep."

She said, "Paul was twenty-eight. He had a lot of trouble with his insides. It was a bad condition and he had no business getting in fights. But he was always fighting. He never had any friends, because he was so hard to get along with. He was sick inside all the time, and he was always irritable and always as nasty as he could be. But I guess that isn't the point. The point is, he always took care of me."

Hart said, "How old are you, Myrna?"

"I'm twenty-six. Paul always treated me as if I was much younger and he was much older. I've been sitting here most of the night thinking of all the things he did for me. He did all those things without ever smiling. When he gave me things or when he did things for me he never smiled and he acted as if he didn't really want to do it. I never knew that was put on. My father used to drink anything he could get his hands on, hair tonic and furniture polish and all that. One night he doubled up and dropped dead. My mother packed up her things and walked out and left us there. Charley came and took care of us. Then Charley had to do a five-year stretch and me and Paul, we had to go to a home. Then Charley was out and one night he came to the home and gave somebody some cash and he took Paul and me away. To look at Charley you'd never think he was past fifty, except for the white hair. Did you ever get so you just wanted to sit alone all by yourself and try to think what's going to happen to you?"

"I get that way once in a while," Hart said. "Not often."

"I looked in the back room," Myrna said, "but Paul wasn't there. What did they do with Paul?"

"I don't know," Hart said.

"I'll find out in the morning," Myrna said. She came out of the chair, toward Hart. The pale blue light rolled over her head and showed her face. In a frail sort of way it was an out-of-the-ordinary face. The eyes were pearly violet. The eyes were ninety-nine percent of her.

She went past Hart and up the stairway. Hart turned off the lamp, groped his way to the stairway, groped his way up and down the hall and into the middle room. A few minutes after he hit the cot he was asleep.

Hart was awake at half past nine. He saw Rizzio moving around the room. He saw Charley still asleep in the wide bed. He turned over and went back to sleep, and at half-past eleven Charley was talking to him, asking him if he wanted to get up. He got out of bed, sat on the edge of the cot until Charley came out of the bathroom. As Charley took off the bathrobe, Hart took a good look at him.

Charley was about five-nine and on the thin side. The silver hair was thick, coming up from a low, unworried forehead, parted in the middle, combed back obliquely, then brushed smooth without benefit of water or oil. The eyes were light blue, nicely spaced above a short, firm nose. The lips were a puzzle, firm and at the same time relaxed, and the skin of the face was beige remaining from a summer's deep tanning.

Charley said, "Why are you sizing me up?"

"I'm curious to see if I can wear your clothes," Hart said.

"What's wrong with your clothes?"

"The suit will do," Hart said, "but I like to wear fresh linen every day."

"Look in the bureau," Charley said. "The three top drawers are mine. You're welcome to whatever you find that fits. You can throw the dirty clothes in the laundry box in the bathroom. I'm going to make you a gift of something I got in the bureau. My skin's too tender and I never got the knack of it, but maybe you'll like it."

Charley opened the top drawer and took out a tan calf-skin case, opening it to show a foreign-make hollow ground safety razor. There was an intricate stropping arrangement where the blade was, and Hart picked up the gadget and said, "Much obliged."

He walked into the bathroom, carrying the tan calfskin case.

Forty minutes later Frieda knocked on the bathroom door and said, "What are your plans?"

Hart had a towel around his middle and the bathroom was filled with steam from very hot water going out of the tub. He said, "I'll be out in a few minutes."

"There's breakfast for you when you come down," Frieda said.

"I'll be right down," Hart said.

Twenty minutes later he came downstairs wearing the chocolate brown suit and his own shoes. He wore Charley's white two-piece underwear and Charley's black silk hose with a green clock, Charley's white shirt, Charley's white starched collar, Charley's black tie with small green polka dots, Charley's white handkerchief in the breast pocket, and Charley's silver cuff links with jade facing.

Rizzio looked up from the sports section and looked at Hart. Then Rizzio, wearing a bathrobe and slippers, extended a flat palm toward Hart while looking at Charley and Mattone, who were reading other sections of the paper in other sections of the living room. And Rizzio said, "Look at this, look at this."

Mattone raised his head from Ed Sullivan's column, glanced at Hart and went back to Sullivan.

Charley looked up from the fourth page and examined Hart and nodded slowly. "I thought it was about the right fit," he said. "Where did you find the cuff links?"

"In the second drawer, way in the back, under some handkerchiefs."

Charley smiled. "I've been looking for those cuff links more than a year. I got them out of an estate in Chestnut Hill. Frieda's got breakfast for you."

Mattone raised his head again and looked at Charley.

Hart walked into the kitchen. Frieda was wearing the quilted robe of orchid satin. Myrna was at the sink, wearing a plain dress of checkered blue and yellow cotton.

Frieda put a tall glass of orange juice on the table and smiled at Hart and said, "Look, honey, there's got to be some stipulation about that bathroom."

"Was I in there long?" Hart said. He lifted the glass.

"It depends on what you call long," Frieda said. "What do you do in there?"

"Dream," Hart said. "But I'll cut it out. All I want is toast and coffee. Black. I'll be right back." He went out and came back seconds later with a lighted cigarette in his mouth.

Frieda said, "I fix up a banquet for him and all he wants is toast and coffee."

"I never eat more than that," Hart said. "My usual meal in the morning is six or seven cigarettes and three or four cups of black coffee without sugar. But if you've prepared something I'll eat it."

He finished the orange juice. Frieda was putting hot dishes on the table. He smiled at her. She walked back to the stove. When she came back to the table she poured coffee with her right hand and with her left hand she reached over and put a soft fat palm over Hart's mouth and with her soft fat fingers she gave his face a soft squeeze.

Myrna was placing dishes in a wall cabinet.

Hart lowered his head and began to eat his meal. Frieda put an ashtray in front of him. He balanced the cigarette on the ashtray and the smoke went up in front of his face as he ate slowly. Frieda and Myrna were moving around in the kitchen. Outside it was beginning to snow. The snow came down haphazardly at first, the flakes gradually forming a pattern as they came streaming down from a dismal grey sky, then all at once parading in thick white columns, an army of white, with limitless reserves. Hart asked Frieda for another cup of coffee, and he sat there sipping the coffee and watching the snow. All at once he sensed that Frieda was no longer in the kitchen. He turned and looked at Myrna. She was on her knees, reaching for something in the floor opening of the wall cabinet.

Hart said, "Hello, Myrna."

She turned and stood up and took two steps going backward. Her eyes were focused on the wall behind his head. She said, "Look, you. I don't want you to talk to me."

Hart took another gulp of coffee, got up and walked out of the kitchen. When he came into the living room he asked Rizzio for another cigarette.

"Let's have some radio," Mattone said.

Hart reached over and turned on the radio. A woman was weeping and a gentle elderly man was saying, "Now, now, Emily—"

Hart tried another station. A crisp young man was saying, "And Ladies, if you've never tried it you don't know what you've missed. Really, Ladies—"

Hart turned off the radio.

Rizzio peeled some pages from the section he was reading and handed the pages to Hart, and Hart tried to concentrate on the rapid progress of a young colored welterweight from Scranton and the boy from Pittsburgh this Scranton boy was slated to meet next week, and also on the card was a promising lightweight from Detroit; and Hart felt the quiet of the living room, the essence of something heavier than the quiet. He started to put down the paper so that he could get a look at Charley and Mattone and Rizzio, and when the paper was halfway down he saw that Charley and Mattone and Rizzio were watching him.

He started to read about how Temple had played a game of basketball with Penn State and the game went into several overtime periods. He liked basketball and at Penn he had played on one of the intramural teams, and this write-up should have interested him even if he had other things on his mind, but it didn't interest him.

He started to lower the paper again, bringing it to one side so he could get a look.

Then he looked and he saw them watching him, and he gazed back at them, one at a time, and finally brought his gaze to rest on Charley.

He was waiting for some sort of a break or a sign, and Charley wasn't giving him anything. He knew he was getting angry, and he sat there wondering whether it would be wise to get angry, or wise to try and stay calm in the face of a colder calm.

Finally Charley broke it. Charley said, "We were talking it over a little while ago. We thought maybe you were going to change your mind."

"Look," Hart said, and he stood up. "If I was going to change my mind I wouldn't let you know about it. I'd just pick myself up and walk out. Even then you wouldn't have anything to worry about, because I wouldn't gain anything by making speeches to the police or anybody. But that's a side issue. The main issue is your point of view, and it's up to you to decide whether I'm in or I'm out. If I'm in it's got to be all the way in. If I'm out you might as well tell me now and I'll leave the neighborhood."

"Don't get all upset," Charley said.

"I'm not upset. I'm just damned curious, that's all."

"That's understandable," Charley said. "It works both ways, we're curious about you and you're curious about us."

And Hart said, "What was it with Renner?"

Mattone turned to Charley and said, "Now do you see what's happening?"

Charley didn't hear what Mattone said. Charley looked at Hart and said, "We did away with Renner because he became greedy. His share of our last job was twelve hundred. He knew where I had the rest of the money and he did a sneak caper, took the eleven thousand and waited thirty minutes and then told me he wanted to buy something on Germantown Avenue. I already knew he had the money, so I took Paul and we went out and did away with him."

"That makes sense," Hart said.

"Sure it does," Charley murmured. Then he grinned. "What say we stop this talk and play some poker?"

They set up a card table, pulled chairs around it and sat

down. Then Rizzio fanned a pack of cards on the table, scooped up the cards, riffled them, fanned them again, caressed them, tossed them up, turned them over, smacked then flat on the table and indicated them for a cut.

Charley cut the cards as he sat down.

"Open," Mattone said. "Quarter, half and seventy-five."

Frieda came in from the kitchen. She sat down at the table.

Rizzio picked up the deck, riffled the cards four times and extended them for another cut.

Charley again cut the cards.

Hart smiled and said, "I'll be a spectator."

"No," Charley said. "You did some work last night in the cellar. You get paid for that work. What do you think it was worth?"

"Around thirty," Hart said.

Charley took out some bills and selected three tens.

"Open," Mattone said. "Quarter, half and—"

"No," Frieda said. "Why should anybody get hurt? Make it closed poker, jacks or better to open the pot, nickel up and dime to open."

Frieda was sitting across from Hart and she smiled at him and he smiled back. Charley asked Rizzio for a cigarette and Rizzio got up from the table, ran upstairs and came down with three packs of cigarettes. He tossed the packs on the table, then eagerly gathered up the cards, riffled them, fanned them in a straight line, riffled them as he watched the others putting their money on the table, fanned the cards in a half-circle, then fanned them in a full circle, a perfect circle, then cut them swiftly three times, held them in front of Hart and told him to take one.

Hart took one, shuffled the deck, cut the deck, and while he was cutting it again Rizzio grinned and said, "All right, your card was a lady, right?"

"So far."

"A black lady."

"Right."

"A black lady in clubs," Rizzio said as he lit a cigarette.

"Right," Hart said, noticing that the others were busy lighting cigarettes and arranging change and bills on the table.

Rizzio riffled the cards, extended the deck to Hart, and Hart cut the cards.

At the end of an hour Hart was winning ten dollars.

At the end of three hours Hart was down to a dollar sixty-five.

When the game ended at five fifteen the following morning, Hart had won three hundred and twenty dollars. Frieda was ahead about fifty, Charley was even, and Mattone and Rizzio were having a dull argument. They were blaming each other for progressively suggesting raising the ante.

Next morning they slept late, started another poker game at three in the afternoon, finished it at four in the morning. This time Hart dropped sixty from his winnings, Frieda was a heavy loser and Charley was even again. On the following day Hart climbed out of bed at two in the afternoon. When he came downstairs be didn't see Charley or Mattone or Rizzio. He didn't see Myrna, either. He went into the kitchen where Frieda was mixing batter for a cake. She had her back turned to him and without looking up from what she was doing she told him to sit down and she'd serve him some breakfast.

He seated himself at the white-topped table. Lighting a cigarette, he said, "Don't fix anything. Just give me black coffee."

She went to the stove and put a fire under the percolator.

The morning paper was on the table and he picked it up and glanced at the front page. An airliner had crashed in the Mediterranean, no survivors. In downtown Philadelphia a stockbroker had tossed himself out of the ninth-floor window of his hotel. In City Hall the District Attorney was blaming the current wave of juvenile delinquency on television and the movies. A local theatre-owner was blaming the current wave of juvenile delinquency on the negligence of the District Attorney. Hart turned the pages and came to the sports section. He looked at a picture of Kid Gavilan in training camp. Alongside the picture there was an interview with the Kid's manager.

Frieda poured coffee and put the cup in front of Hart. Then she stepped back and looked him over. He sat there and felt the pressure of her eyes. There was heat in the pressure and he started to wonder what her plans were. He told himself to let it ride, he didn't need anything she had, he didn't go for the meaty bulging type, and besides, a situation with Frieda would only complicate a set-up that was already damn well complicated.

"You look good today," Frieda said.

"Thanks."

The chocolate-brown flannel was holding up fairly well, and under it he wore one of Charley's high-priced white shirts and an olive-green tie with yellow diagonal stripes. His face was mowed smooth and his hair, although brushed dry, was a glimmering yellow. He had it brushed flat and smooth and Frieda put her fat hand on it, her palm gliding lightly across his head.

"Maybe I'll muss it up," Frieda said.

"I wish you wouldn't."

"Why not?"

"You might get excited."

"What's wrong with that?" Frieda asked.

"I think it might create a problem."

"Yeah?" Frieda spoke quietly. "That's one kind of problem I can always handle."

He looked at her. "You sure?"

She nodded solemnly.

"I wonder," he murmured.

"Don't let it bother you," Frieda said. "Let me take care of it. When I'm ready for you, I'll let you know."

He smiled slightly. He snapped his fingers. "Just like that?"

"Yeah." She snapped her fingers. "Just like that."

He told himself to change the subject. Turning his attention to the coffee, he said, "Where're the others?"

"Charley went out with Mattone and Rizzio. They're casing some real estate in Wyncote."

"And Myrna?"

"She's out shopping."

He waited a long moment, then said slowly, "You sent her out?"

"That's right," Frieda said. She put a little pause between each word. "I sent her out."

He was still trying to change the subject and he said, "How come Charley went out? I thought he'd stay inside a few more days. This neighborhood's still hot."

"It's cooled off a little," Frieda said. She picked up the newspaper, turned the pages and came to page four. Her finger pointed to a small headline near the bottom of the page.

Hart glanced through the story. It was about Renner. It said the body of the man found shot in Germantown had been identified as that of Frederick Renner, a former convict, wanted for skipping parole and suspected of several recent burglaries. Police said Renner was probably shot by a personal enemy or a business competitor. The tone of the story indicated that Renner's death was no loss to the public and the police wouldn't be knocking themselves out searching for the slayer.

"It looks like an all-clear," Hart said. "But then, the police are funny. You never know what they'll do."

"Charley knows," Frieda said. "They never fool Charley."

"Never?" He had it down near a whisper.

"That's what I said. Never. And that applies to other people, too. There's nobody can fool Charley. Not for long, anyway."

He decided to let it pass. Then he had a feeling he ought to take her up on that. She was getting at something and if it was going to come out, it might as well come out now.

He said, "Could you fool Charley?"

"I'd be crazy to try." She'd gone back to the shelf near the sink and she was busy again with the cake batter.

Hart waited a few moments and then he said, "What about me? You think I could fool him?"

As he said it, he was lifting the coffee cup to his mouth. He sipped the coffee and the only sound he heard was the gooey stirring of the wooden spoon in the batter bowl. The stirring went on and he sipped more coffee. Then he finished the cup and leaned back and lit a cigarette. And the sound of the stirring went on and on. He told himself she wasn't going to answer.

Then he heard her saying, "What do you think?"

"I'm asking you," he said.

She turned very slowly. "I'll tell you," she said. "If you were a mixture of Houdini and Thurston and the world's champion chess player, card shark and con man, your chances of fooling Charley would be one in a million."

"You quoting odds?"

"Sure as hell," Frieda nodded. "If I had a million I'd put it on Charley against your dollar bill."

"Without worrying?"

"Without a moment's thought."

He took a long drag from the cigarette. He let it out slowly. "Well," he murmured. "Well, now. That's very interesting."

"Yeah," Frieda said. She turned back to the cake batter. "It's something for you to think about. But don't let it throw you."

I'll try not to, he said without sound. But a tiny frown appeared on his brow and began to grow. He took a tighter drag from the cigarette and hauled it down deep. He told his brain to pull away from Charley and think about Kid Gavilan or the British airliner. Or anything at all that would detour the worry. But the thing is, he said to himself, it's definitely something to worry about. It's what every living thing is constantly facing up against, the problem of staying alive. Except with you it's a matter of an inch here, an inch there, one wrong move, like with those German acrobats you saw not long ago in a picture magazine, they were walking a tightrope stretched between two peaks in the Alps, and under them was some six thousand feet of nothing. Well, what the hell, it might just as well have been six hundred feet. Or sixty feet. You fall sixty feet, you'll wind up in a casket just the same. And when they close the lid, it doesn't make any difference how you passed out, whether it was falling off the rope or down a flight of stairs or pneumonia or typhoid or going to sleep with the gas on. There now, that's getting us away from this Charley business. You think so? You mean, you hope so. I'll tell you something, though. It would be much easier if you didn't give a hang whether you lived to be ninety or thirty-five. Fact is, you do give a hang. So maybe the only move to make is get up from this chair and stroll out the door and keep strolling. Sure, that would be a smart move. Extremely brilliant, just like jumping into a vat of boiling hot oil, with some rookie policemen reaching in to pull you out and take you in and get their promotion. So the slogan for today is: Stay put, leave well enough alone. Just keep it in mind that you're sitting in a chair that's not electric but if you walk out you're headed for a piece of furniture that's strictly from high voltage. You might as well have another cup of coffee and another cigarette and more pleasant chatting with Frieda. That's some rear end she has there. Like a Cadillac. If she weighed some fifty pounds less you might be inclined to play around a little, just to kill time. But all that weight, that's not your speed.

"More coffee?" Frieda asked.

He nodded, and she gave him another cup. The batter was in the pan and the pan was in the oven, so now for a while she could sit down and rest. She took a chair at the table facing him, helped herself to one of his cigarettes, picked up his book of matches and lit it. He had his head lowered to get at the coffee in the cup, but in the instant before he sipped it, he ventured a glance at her face, aiming at her eyes, seeing what was in her eyes and knowing in that same instant that she was having trouble.

He knew there was something she wanted to tell him. It was something she wasn't allowed to tell him and she was very anxious to say it and so there she was with her problem. Well, whatever it was, it wouldn't come out of her unless he pulled it out. And the only way to pull it out was slow and easy, very careful.

The coffee cup was half empty before he spoke. He set the cup in the saucer and said, "I've been thinking what you said about Charley."

"Yeah," sort of sadly, regretfully. "I shouldn't of told you that."

"I'm glad you did."

"Why?" She leaned forward just a little. "Why are you glad?"

He shrugged. "It lets me know the score. It always helps to know the score."

"You think you got the complete picture?"

He didn't reply. His face didn't show anything. He was telling himself this was the only way to handle it.

She opened her mouth, closed it, opened it again, bit her lip as though trying to bite on the words to keep them from coming out. She said, "Let me tell you something—"

But then her lips were clamped tightly and she stared past him as though looking at a traffic light flashing red.

He spoke mildly, not too casually, just casual enough. "What is it? You want me for a boy friend? Is that what's bothering you?"

Her tone was matter-of-fact. "It happens I already got a boy friend."

"Mattone?"

"No," she said. "No, for Christ's sake. What made you think of Mattone?"

"He's very good looking."

"I wouldn't know. I've never gandered him that close. Only thing I'd wanna put on him is spit."

"What about Rizzio?"

She laughed dryly. "Rizzio's one for the books. I mean the kind of books you gotta buy in foreign countries, they're outlawed here."

"Well, like they always say, to each his own."

"Yeah, it's a good phrase." She said it as though there was something sour in her mouth. "Only trouble is, for some people it's more wishing than having. The one I got—"

And again she was biting her lip.

He said, "Is it Charley?"

She nodded.

"You don't really want him?"

"Sure I want him." She said it emphatically, sort of angrily. "I really go for him. And it's vice versa, he'd do anything for me. That is, anything he can do. But there's something the matter with his machinery and he can't."

"Never?"

She spoke dully, in the resigned tone of someone burdened with a blind or crippled relative. "Sometimes he drinks himself into a condition where he don't know what he's doing and then, somehow . . ."

"Well, that's something."

"Yeah, it's marvelous. It happens maybe once every three months."

He frowned slightly. "Say, that's no joke."

"You're wrong there," she said. "It's a big joke. It's gotta be a laugh, and Charley and me, we laugh about it all the time. If I didn't laugh—" she almost choked on the words, "—I'd flip my lid sure as hell."

"Would he care if you—?"

"No, he wouldn't care. If he's told me once, he's told me a hundred times to go out when I need it. As if it's a high-colonic, or something like that. He really means it, he ain't pulling my leg or testing my loyalty. He really wants me to have it, he says it's bad for my health to go without it too long."

Hart nodded seriously. "He's got something there."

She didn't say anything. She was staring at the table top.

"Well," Hart said, "it's no problem to get it on the outside. The streets are filled with men who'd be only too willing. You have the face, you have the body—"

"Sure, I know. I used to go for long walks and they'd give me the eye and then we'd get to talking. With a few of them I'd wind up having a drink somewhere. But that's as far as it would go. I'd always start thinking about Charley."

"Feeling guilty?"

She shook her head. "Nothing like that. Just comparing Charley with these four-star jerks, these absolute nothings. I swear, there wasn't one of them could budge me an inch. They had the looks, the clothes, the smooth approach, but underneath it was zero, no ignition."

"That isn't their fault. It's Charley. You're all wrapped up with Charley. He's got you paralyzed."

She sent a smile past him. "You think so?"

He shrugged. "It figures." Then a carefully-timed pause. And then, "Wouldn't you say it figures?"

The smile faded. She went on looking past him. "I don't know," she said. "I'm trying to see it. Get it added up. It's kind of hazy, it won't build. Something's in my head and it's Charley's face, the sound of his voice, the way he moves around, Jesus Christ, that's what's blocking me, I can't get the bastard out of my head—"

Hart told himself to keep his mouth shut.

Frieda lowered her head and pressed her hands to the sides of her face. She began to breathe hard. She started to lift her head, then forced it down. And suddenly she shivered as though a chunk of ice was applied to the back of her neck. Her hands came down hard on the table top and again she lifted her head and her eyes took hold of Hart.

"You," she said. "You've done it."

He sat there passively, waiting.

"You've done what none of the others could do," she said. "You've sent Charley away for awhile."

His lips scarcely moved. "Have I? You sure?"

It seemed there was flame coming out of her face. She stood up and said, "I'll prove it."

He saw her moving toward him. He felt her hand on his wrist, her fingers sliding across his knuckles and entwining with his fingers.

He heard her saying, "Come on, let's go upstairs."

He sat there at the kitchen table and heard her saying it again. He was telling himself to sit there and not move a muscle. Now she was pulling at his arm and he smiled dimly and let his arm go limp. She gave a hard pull but in that instant he stiffened it and she felt the resistance.

She let go and stepped back and said, "What's the matter?"

"Nothing."

"Look at me," she said.

He looked at her. She had her hands on her bulging hips, her big breasts heaved and quivered. She spoke thickly. "Didn't you hear what I said? I said I'm ready."

"I heard you," he murmured.

"Come on," she said. "Come on, come on."

He didn't move. He went on looking at her. There was no expression on his face.

She gave him a side-glance, a frown getting started and deepening. "You want me to put it in writing or something? I'm telling you I'm ready."

"But I'm not."

She took another backward step. She blinked several times. Her lips scarcely moved as she said, "I don't get this."

"Add it up," he said.

"Add what?" She was near shrieking. "What's there to add?"

He didn't reply.

She was trying to calm down. She managed to breathe slower, and her voice quieted as she said, "What is it? Tell me. Let's get this straightened out."

"I wish we could," he said. He made it sound very soft and sincere. "I really wish we could."

She moved toward the table, pulled a chair close to him and sat down. She leaned forward and took hold of his hands. "Tell me," she said. "What's bothering you?"

"The blues," he said. He arranged a sad smile on his face. "I got the blues."

Frieda frowned again. "What do you mean? What kind of blues?"

"The time element," he said. "Let's call it the Calendar Blues."

She waited for him to explain that.

He said, "It goes something like this. You want me to show you a good time. You want us to go upstairs and have ourselves some fun. Well, that's all right. There's nothing wrong with that. Except I'm just not up to it. I'm thinking in terms of the calendar and how many days I'll stay alive."

She winced slightly. She gave him a side-glance and said, "That's a happy thought."

"Can't help it. It's there."

"But why? What makes you think—?"

"It's the situation," he said. "I'm here in this house like merchandise sold on a time-trial. If I meet the requirements, I'm in. If not—" He shrugged.

Frieda's eyes narrowed just a little. "You worried you won't make the grade?"

He didn't answer. He knew it was time to let her do the talking.

She said, "I can't give you no guarantees, only way I can put it is I'm betting you'll be around a long time. When you first came here I wouldn't of given a dime for your chances. But then I watched your stock going up with Charley. For instance, that overcoat business. You said you stole the coat and Mattone called you a liar, so Charley phoned the store and sure enough the coat was hot. That was something. That put you on first base."

He shrugged again. "It's a long trip to home plate."

"I think you're getting there," she said.

He waited. He wondered if it would come now.

And then he heard her saying, "What really sent your stock way up was that deal with the wallet, when you came back and handed him the money. That made a big hit with Charley. Another thing. The thing with Paul. When you helped Charley to put him in the furnace. You did what Rizzio couldn't do, what Mattone couldn't do. I think that put you safe on third."

Now he could feel it coming and he had to restrain himself to keep from leaning forward expectantly.

"So what it amounts to," she said, "you're gradually proving you can meet the requirements. You're getting it across that you're really a professional."

And there it was. She'd given him the tip-off he'd been waiting for. She told him he would stay alive just as long as Charley had him checked and approved as a true-blue outlaw.

She said, "You get the drift? That's the big thing, that professional angle. Because we're strictly professional and we ain't got room here for no amateurs."

There was the slightest trace of challenge in the way she said it. He could see her eyes getting narrow again. He said to himself, Don't underestimate the brains of this girl; that head of hers is no empty tool box.

Frieda was saying, "You told Charley you're wanted for murder in New Orleans. You told him the set-up, what you did and why you did it and maybe by this time he's bought your story. Unless, of course—"

He waited for her to go on. She was looking at him and her eyes remained narrow.

"Unless what?" he murmured.

"Maybe you're bluffing."

He frowned.

"If you're bluffing," she said, "it's a cinch Charley's

gonna find out. Like I told you, it just ain't possible to fool Charley."

He erased the frown. There was nothing special on his face as he said, "I gave him a few facts, that's all. A few straight facts. It happened in New Orleans, it was my brother who died, it was me who did it, and it was murder."

"You said you did it for money," she said. "And that makes it professional. If you'd done it for any other reason, it wouldn't have been professional. Most murders are strictly hate jobs. Or love jobs. Or something you do when you go crazy for a minute and then you're sorry. But when it's done for money it's purely a business transaction, it puts you in a special bracket, it makes you really a professional."

He thought: She's got me, she set the trap very nicely and I'll be damned if she hasn't got me.

"The way it stacks up," she said, "the fact you murdered somebody, that ain't important to Charley. Or who you murdered. Or the way you did it. Only thing Charley wants to know is why you did it. So you tell him you did it for money. And if he buys that, you're safe, you got a membership card, you're really in. But on the other hand, if he finds out you didn't do it for the money—"

"You think I was bluffing about that?"

"I don't think anything," Frieda said. "All I'm saying is, if you told him the truth you got nothing to worry about. And if there's nothing to worry about, there's no reason to have the blues."

"You're right." He grinned. "They're gone away. No more blues."

She grinned back at him. "You sure?"

He nodded slowly.

She got up from the chair. "Well," she said, "I'm still in that same condition. I'm ready."

He stood up. "So am I."

She moved toward him and put her arm around his middle. His hand settled on the solid fat meat of her hip. The only feeling he had was the feeling of taking a ride he didn't want to take. But the thing to do was take it and like it, or anyway try to make her believe he was liking it. He thought: This is a very hungry woman and she won't settle for anything less than a first-class job. You disappoint her, you'll really be singing the blues. She's found the loophole in your New Orleans news item and all she needs to do is put a little bug in Charley's ear and next on the agenda is he does some checking and discovers you told him just one tiny untruth, you said you murdered your brother for money and Christ knows it wasn't for money, so when Charley finds out you're not a professional it's definitely the wind-up, he'll give you a kindly smile, a gentle good-bye, he'll put the bullet in you very quick and merciful. Well, all right then, we'll try to handle it so it won't wind up that way. We'll try to keep Frieda happy. It's sure taking us a long time to get upstairs. That's your fault, you're walking too slow. Let's negotiate these stairs a little faster. Another thing, let's give her a smile, get it sort of hot and eager, come on, put it across like they do in the movies when it's just pretending but they gotta make it seem real, like the way they do it when they're aiming for an Academy Award, but then if they don't get it they can try again next year, the lucky bastards, but for you it's just this one try and if you don't make good it's all options dropped, everything dropped, everything finished. Well now, here we are upstairs in the hall and there's the bedroom. Let's stop here just a moment or so and hold her a little tighter, let's give it some preliminary action, a blazing kiss deep to her mouth to let her know what's coming later. Well, that wasn't bad. Looks as though she liked that.

Frieda was taking off her clothes as they entered the room.

It was a few hours later and Hart sat on the couch in the living room, reading a comic magazine. There was nothing else to read. Soon Charley came in with Mattone and Rizzio.

Their overcoats were flecked with snow. They took off the coats, doing it slowly, somewhat tiredly. Hart guessed they'd had a busy afternoon. Rizzio said, "I'm gonna take a nap before dinner," and he went upstairs. Mattone waited a few moments, then said, "I'll get some shut-eye, too," and moved toward the couch. Hart got up and took a chair on the other side of the room. Charley stood in the middle of the floor, pulling a folded sheet of paper from the inside pocket of his suit. He unfolded the paper and stood there reading some penciled notations and a roughly drawn diagram. From where Hart was sitting it was possible to see the diagram. It showed the exterior of a large mansion and the surrounding estate, with tennis courts and a stable and a four-car garage.

Some moments passed, and then without saying a word Charley came toward him and handed him the sheet of paper. Hart leaned back in the chair, puffing gently at the cigarette, seeing what was on the paper but not getting anything from it, getting only the soft but steady pressure from Charley's eyes aiming at his face. He knew that Charley was looking for a reaction and he told himself the best reaction was no reaction at all.

For the better part of a minute he continued to focus on the diagram and the notes. Then, looking up at Charley, making it quiet and technical, "This looks very juicy."

Charley nodded. "The Kenniston estate. Ever hear of the Kennistons?"

Hart made a negative gesture.

"Society people," Charley said. "They really have it. Let's say around thirty, forty million. They got a lot of it invested in art treasures. Mostly oriental stuff, like jade and rose quartz and ivory. You familiar with that material?"

"A little," Hart said. "When'd you pick up on this?"

"Couple months ago. They loaned the collection to the Parkway Museum for a three-week exhibit. I went down and had a look at it. Mostly small items, about the size of your thumb. In terms of antique value it amounts to a big haul. Some of them things go back two, three thousand years."

Hart looked at the sheet of paper. He didn't say anything.

Charley went on, "As it stands now, it's around a million dollars' worth of goods. If we get it, I figure it'll bring around three fifty."

"That's high," Hart said. He wondered if it sounded professional.

"Yeah, I know it sounds high," Charley said. "But there's a hungry market for this kind of merchandise. They lost it ages ago and now they want it back."

"China?"

"Red China."

"Through what channel?"

"They got some people working here," Charley said. "They got other people in South America. And some in the islands. It goes from one place to another until it gets to China."

Hart glanced again at the sheet of paper. He said softly, very softly, "Three hundred and fifty grand."

"At least that," Charley murmured. He gestured toward the paper. "You like the layout?"

"I don't know yet," Hart said carefully, but with the feeling he was saying the wrong thing. And then, to himself, What else could you say?

Charley was saying, "We do it Friday. It's gonna be Friday night."

Without sound Hart said: Today is Wednesday. It's Wednesday and then comes Thursday and then Friday.

His eyes hit the diagram on the paper and stayed there and then it seemed the penciled drawing of the mansion was rising from the paper and moving toward his face. Then it was really the interior of the mansion and they were in there going for the art treasures, he was doing everything wrong and demonstrating his lack of professional acumen. Charley watched him and smiled at him and when they were outside and in the car, Charley showed him the gun and gave him a final smile and then shot him.

Friday, Hart thought. He remembered the dateline on today's *Inquirer.* It was January 11. So Friday would be the 13th. It had a black sound and he was telling himself that Friday would be a black day. But maybe not. Maybe if he could—

"The hell with it," he said aloud.

"What?" Charley murmured. "What's that?"

He grinned at Charley. He said, "I was thinking, some people are superstitious. I mean about Friday the thirteenth."

Charley was quiet for a long moment. He looked down at the carpet. He said, "Are you superstitious?"

"No," Hart said.

"Neither am I." Charley turned and gestured toward the couch where Mattone was sound asleep. "That one is."

"Friday the thirteenth," Hart said. "They call it Black Friday. You think he'll worry about that?"

"Let him worry. He's always worrying, anyway. Not a day passes he don't find something to worry about."

"All right." Hart gave a slight shrug. "It's all right with me."

Charley looked past him. "I wonder."

Hart grinned again. "I told you I wasn't superstitious."

"Yes, you told me." Charley went on looking past him. "You been telling me a lot of things. The more things you tell me, the more I wonder?"

Hart held onto the grin, twisted it just a little, and said, "If you don't like it, Charley, you know what you can do."

Charley looked at him. For a very long moment Charley didn't speak. Then softly, "Maybe I don't know what to do. You wanna tell me what to do?"

The grin stayed there. And his voice was just as soft as Charley's. "You can go to hell, that's what."

"You kidding?"

"No, I'm not kidding," Hart said. "You called me a liar and I told you where to go."

"Don't get worked up," Charley said. "I didn't call you a liar."

"Look, Charley." He stood up. "I don't like to be insulted. You can dish it out to Mattone, to Rizzio, to anyone you choose. If they wanna take it, that's their business. But I won't take it. I never take it from anybody and I'm not taking it from you."

Charley inclined his head and gave Hart a slow up-and-down look. "Tell me something—" It was almost a whisper. "What are you trying to get across?"

"You want me to say it again?"

"Just say what you really mean."

"That's another insult." Hart's mouth scarcely moved. "You're piling them up, Charley."

Again Charley gave him the slow up-and-down and then he said, "It's too bad. I didn't think we'd have this. I was getting to like you."

There was a trace of honest sadness in Charley's tone. Hart began to feel a stiffness in his spine, he told himself he'd taken it maybe a little too far. Somewhere between his spine and his brain he could hear Frieda's voice again and she was saying: You can't fool Charley.

He heard Charley saying, "I actually figured we'd get to be chums."

Hart grinned again. "Go fishing together?"

"And skiing. I've always wanted to try skis but I never had anybody to go with. You know, it's lousy when you don't have a chum. Last time I had a real chum, I think I was twelve years old."

"But now, like the Bible says, it's time to put away child-ish things."

"You're so right," Charley said. "When you grow up it's a cold world and the only thing you can trust is an adding machine."

It was an opening, and Hart plunged into it. "I'm not ask-ing you to trust me, Charley. I don't trust myself, not com-pletely anyway. It all depends on the time and the place. I might pull a caper next month I wouldn't do today. But that's for the future, and what we're dealing with now is now. I have no plans for now except to be on your payroll and do what you say."

"Only for now," Charley mused. "That's putting things on a short-term contract."

"It's the best I can offer," Hart said. It sounded genuine and as the words came out he knew it wouldn't need more words.

Charley said, "You know something, Al? I think you made a sale there."

Hart shrugged. He pressed his cigarette into an ashtray. His other hand held the sheet of paper that showed the Kenniston estate in Wyncote. He looked down at the dia-gram of the mansion and frowned slightly and said, "Is this according to scale?"

"Not hardly," Charley said. "But I think you can estimate some fifty yards to each half-inch. From the gate to the front entrance it looks to be some fifteen hundred yards."

"That's a long walk."

"Yeah," Charley murmured dryly. "It might be a long run."

"They got dogs?"

"We saw two," Charley said. "They were big ones. Bad ones. But that won't be no problem, we got ourselves a dog expert, Rizzio. He's really an expert with dogs."

"What are these dogs?"

"Dobermans."

"He'd better be an expert," Hart said.

From the kitchen, Frieda was shouting, "Come on in, dinner's ready."

The six of them were seated at the table in the small dining room. They'd had tomato juice and now they were eating T-bone steak and salad with French dressing. It was a fine steak, cooked medium-rare and they were all busy with it.

Hart sat next to Rizzio, the two women sat across from him, and Mattone and Charley faced each other from the opposite ends of the table. Mattone was eating with his head down close to the plate and suddenly he raised his head and glowered at the table. Then he glowered at Frieda.

"What's the matter?" Frieda asked, her mouth crammed with steak and salad and buttered roll.

"Where's the A-1 sauce?" Mattone demanded.

"Look in the kitchen," Frieda said. "On the shelf near the icebox."

Mattone looked at Myrna. "Get it for me."

"Get it yourself," Myrna said.

She said it very quietly. But there was something about the way she said it. They'd all stopped eating and they were looking at her.

"Get me the A-1 sauce," Mattone said. "And I'm not gonna ask you again."

"That's all right with me," Myrna said.

Mattone put down his knife and fork.

"All right," Charley said. "All right."

"No," Mattone said. "No, Charley. It ain't all right."

Charley looked up at the ceiling. "Get him the sauce," he said.

Myrna didn't move. She had the knife going into her steak while she steadied it with the fork. No one else was eating and they were all watching her as she sliced the steak. She wasn't even looking at the steak. It was hard to tell what she was looking at. And Hart began to have the feeling that her refusal to wait on Mattone had nothing to do with Mattone.

Rizzio pushed back his chair. "I'll get it," he said, and he started to rise. But Mattone pushed him back and said, "You sit there. She'll get it," and then Frieda said, "Aw, the hell with this. I'll get it," but Mattone motioned her to stay where she was. Mattone said, "She's gonna get that bottle of sauce for me, you hear? Her job here is house cleaning and helping with the cooking and waiting on the table. She gets paid for it and she's gonna do it."

Mattone's mouth was clamped very tightly and he was looking at Myrna. He had his hands gripping the edge of the table, his knuckles white and getting whiter. Charley was watching him, studying him, and then Charley started to get up, but just then Mattone made his move, leaping up and then sideways with his arm shooting out, his fingers closing on Myrna's wrist and twisting hard so that she dropped the knife. But her other hand held onto the fork and as Mattone went on twisting her wrist it seemed she didn't feel the pain, she made no sound, her face was expressionless while she hauled off with the fork and then jabbed it into his arm just below the shoulder.

"Jesus Christ," Mattone screamed. He staggered back, grabbing at his punctured arm. He bumped against his chair, knocked it over, then stumbled over it and went to the floor.

Rizzio was up, Frieda was up, and they helped Mattone off the floor. Charley was looking at Myrna, and Hart was looking at the bloody prongs of the fork in her hand. Now it was quiet in the room and they were removing Mattone's jacket. His shirtsleeve near the shoulder was getting drenched bright red, the blood was coming out fast. His eyes popped as he watched his shirtsleeve getting redder, the stain widening. The injured arm hung loose and his other arm quivered as he started to unbutton his shirt. His fingers fumbled with the buttons and Frieda grunted impatiently, stepped in close, pulled the shirt free of his trousers, got a firm hold on the white broadcloth, and ripped it up the front.

"My shirt," Mattone wailed. "You're tearing my shirt—"

Frieda went on ripping the shirt. She sliced it all the way up the front, then over the shoulder and down the back.

"You've ruined it," Mattone screeched. He sounded almost hysterical. "Imported broadcloth—twenty-three fifty—it was made to measure—"

"Shut up," Frieda said freeing the sleeve from the torn shirt. "Get something," she said to no one in particular. "We got any peroxide?"

"I'll look," Charley said. He gave a slight sigh as he got up from the table.

Frieda had arranged a folded rag from a piece of the torn shirt and she was wiping the blood from Mattone's arm. Mattone was speaking quietly now and his features were calm. He gazed at Myrna and said, "Look what you did. Take a look at my arm."

Myrna didn't seem to hear. She was in her chair again, looking at the knife on her plate. Her face was pale but placid and there was nothing in her eyes. Hart told himself that maybe she'd really cracked and he wondered if there was a way to test her. Or maybe, he thought, you better stay out of it, you're not involved in this. Oh yeah? The hell you're not. You're planted right in the middle, brother, it's you she's really after and you know it and you know why.

He decided to test Myrna's condition and his hand went into his jacket pocket, came out with his cigarettes. He offered her the pack, saying, "Have a smoke?"

But there was no reaction. She continued to look at the knife resting on the plate. Frieda and Rizzio and Mattone were watching, wondering what Hart was trying to prove.

"No peroxide. All we got is iodine." It was Charley coming into the room with iodine and a wet washrag and some Band-Aids. He saw what Hart was doing with the pack of cigarettes and he frowned slightly and murmured, "What's happening now?"

"I think she's sick," Hart said.

"No." It was Mattone. He was grinning loosely and saying, "She ain't sick. You know she ain't sick. You know
what's the matter with her."

Hart didn't reply. Charley handed the washrag and iodine
to Frieda and she applied the wet cloth to the holes in Mattone's arm. Rizzio went back to his chair and resumed eating
his steak. Frieda was busy now with the iodine. It appeared
that Mattone didn't feel the iodine, he was still grinning at
Hart. The Band-Aids were resting on the table and there
were four of them and Frieda was picking them up one by
one and securing them over the holes in Mattone's arm.
Now Charley had returned to his chair and he went back to
where he'd left off with the T-bone on his plate. Frieda com-
pleted her work with the Band-Aids and moved back to her
place next to Myrna, while Mattone stood up and walked
slowly out of the room. Then it was quiet in the room and
they were all eating their steaks and salad, with the excep-
tion of Myrna who continued to sit there with the placid look
on her face, the nothingness in her eyes, her eyes aiming at
the knife. Hart was telling himself to give his undivided
attention to the meat on his plate. But while he chewed on
the steak his brain stalled on him, then stumbled away from
where he was trying to steer it, his thoughts went lurching
and tumbling down an actual flight of stairs to the actual cellar to the actual furnace. He was seeing Myrna's brother getting chopped up and tossed into the furnace. Then he went
back to the moment when his knee had made contact with
Paul, thudding into Paul's groin, doing something to Paul's
insides causing things to go wrong, causing hemorrhage and
then the finish, causing the girl to lose her brother. So what
he'd taken away from her was something that couldn't be
replaced, and now he remembered his talk with Myrna in
the living room the night Paul died and she was dazed then
with the shock of it, the hurt and the hate hadn't yet set in.
And so now, not wanting to look at her, he was forced to
look at her and he saw the small skinny girl with the black
hair and the violet eyes and the pale placid face. Just five-
two, and if the scale showed more than ninety-five pounds
there was something wrong with the scale. She looked so little sitting there. And yet he knew he was looking at trouble,
big trouble, something more threatening than anything else

dangling over his head. He wondered if maybe he could somehow talk to her and—

A blast of music came into the dining room. It was hot jazz jumping out of the radio in the living room, followed by footsteps and then Mattone coming in wearing a fresh shirt and a hand-painted necktie and the same grin he'd worn when he'd walked out. Hart saw the grin was aimed at him and he heard Charley saying, "All right now, Mattone. Cut it out."

"What am I doing?" Mattone asked mildly.

"I said cut it out."

Mattone walked past the table, moving behind Hart, and went into the kitchen. Then he came out of the kitchen and in his hand was the bottle of A-1 sauce. He sat down and poured the sauce on his lukewarm steak. He reached for a roll with his uninjured arm, put a thick dab of butter on the roll. He took a generous bite of the roll, then sliced a big chunk of steak. He shoved the steak into his mouth and chewed energetically and while he did this he was grinning again at Hart.

From the living room there was a trumpet blast climbing high while the drummer banged with all his might on the cymbal, and Rizzio whined, "For Christ's sake. We need all that noise?"

"Leave it on," Mattone said. "It's Dizzy Gillespie. I like Dizzy Gillespie."

"It sounds like someone caught under a steamroller," Frieda said.

"Not exactly," Mattone said. "It ain't like what comes out of the mouth." For some moments the grin was gone, he'd stopped chewing on the steak, he was frowning thoughtfully. And then, "I'll tell you what it is. It's—"

"It's bebop," Rizzio said. "Ain't it bebop?"

"Sure it's bop," Mattone nodded. "But that ain't what I mean. What I mean is—well, when Dizzy takes it way up, gets all the way up there higher than high, he's telling you something, he's putting it to you straight, telling you what it sounds like inside."

"Inside what?" Rizzio asked.

"In here," Mattone said, and he indicated his head and his chest. "You get it?"

"No," Rizzio said.

"Because you're an imbecile," Mattone told him amiably. "It takes someone with brains to understand what I mean. Like our friend here," and he pointed his finger at Hart.

"You starting again?" Charley asked quietly. "Ain't we had enough for one night?"

"I'm just making conversation," Mattone answered. "Sure, our friend here knows what I mean. He knows what she sounds like inside."

"Leave him alone." Charley's voice climbed just a little.

"I'm not bothering him," Mattone said. "It's the girl here. She's bothering him. She's got him worried plenty."

"Oh, for God's sake," Frieda protested. "Do something, Charley. Make him stop."

Charley gave Mattone a very thin-smile. It was on the order of a final warning.

But Mattone had started it and couldn't stop it, the way certain reptiles are biologically unable to stop a meal once the victim's head is in their mouth. Mattone said, "She stabs me with the fork but it's really him she wants to stab. And not in the arm, either."

Charley started to rise from his chair.

But Hart reached out and put his hand on Charley's shoulder. "Sit there," Hart murmured. "Let him talk. I want to hear the rest of this."

"Sure you do," Mattone grinned. "You wanna see if it checks with what you're thinking. Ain't that correct?"

Hart nodded slowly. And now he was looking at Myrna. She had raised her head slightly and her eyes were focused blankly on his chin, or maybe his throat, he wasn't quite sure.

"You see the way it figures?" Mattone asked the other faces at the table. "She has it in for him and she takes it out on me. That happens sometimes, I guess. When they get so mixed up they don't know what they're trying to hit, they hit what's closest. But sooner or later they straighten their aim. It's just a question of time."

"You louse." Frieda gave Mattone a disgusted look.

"Me?" Mattone pointed to himself innocently. "You got it backwards, Frieda. I'm only trying to lend a hand. I'd hate to see him get hurt."

"Yeah," Frieda said. "Yeah. Sure."

"I'm giving him advice, that's all," Mattone said. "Just telling him to be careful. To keep his eyes on her. Watch every move she makes. Or maybe—" he hesitated a moment, then let it slide out, "—he oughta do the safest thing and take off."

It was heavily quiet for some moments. Frieda was looking at Charley, waiting for Charley to get up again and go for Mattone. But Charley didn't move. Charley was watching Myrna. She ended the quiet with the scraping of her chair. Then she was up from the table, going around it very slowly, moving somewhat like a sleepwalker as she went out of the room.

Rizzio said, "Who wants coffee?"

"We'll all have coffee," Frieda said. "You got any poisoned coffee for Mattone?"

Charley looked at Frieda. Then he looked at Hart. Then he gazed at Frieda again, and his head moved in an almost imperceptible nod. "Any liquor?" he asked.

"We got some bourbon and some gin."

"Bring the gin," Charley said.

"What's the matter now?" Mattone was staring from face to face and getting no answer.

"It don't concern you," Charley said. His gaze moved back and forth quickly between Frieda and Hart.

Rizzio came in with the gin. He was frowning, puzzled, because Charley rarely went for gin, went for it only when something happened to knock him off balance and he urgently needed a bracer.

Charley took the bottle and began pouring the gin into a water glass. He got the glass three-quarters full. He lifted the glass to his mouth and drank the gin as though it was water.

The radio was playing more bebop. It was Dizzy Gillespie again and Dizzy's trumpet went up and up and way up.

You'll get sick," Frieda said. She watched the gin flowing from the bottle to the water glass. Charley was on his fourth glass and Hart estimated that Charley had already consumed more than a pint of gin. Mattone had finished his coffee and left the table, and now Rizzio was getting up.

"You're burning up your liver," Frieda said. She was trying to keep her voice down. "It'll be like the last time, you'll hafta have your stomach pumped out."

Charley smiled at Hart. "Want some gin?"

"No thanks," Hart said.

"Don't you like gin?"

"Not especially."

"It's a thin drink," Charley said. His smile was sort of loose. "Not much body to it."

Hart didn't say anything.

"Maybe that's the reason you don't like it," Charley said. "Maybe you like something with more body."

"What's that mean?" Hart asked. He said to himself: You know what it means, all right.

"He means me," Frieda said. She was starting to breathe hard. "Ain't that it, Charley?"

Charley put the smile on Frieda. "You want a drink?"

"No," Frieda said. Now suddenly she was breathing very hard. She looked at Hart. "Go in the other room. You don't figure in this—"

"Not much he don't," Charley said softly. Then he chuckled, but only with his mouth. His eyes were fixed icily on a path going straight ahead at the wall and through the wall. "Way this stacks up, it's a three-sided discussion."

"It don't hafta be," Frieda said. "You're just making it that way."

"No, lady," Charley said. "It's already made. It was made this afternoon, while I was out." And then, after a long pause, "Tell me, lady. How was it?"

"You're not funny, Charley."

"Oh, but you're wrong, lady. You're so wrong. I'm very funny. You wanna know something? I'm the funniest man I've ever met."

"All right," Frieda said. "Drink your gin. Drink it up and get yourself unconscious and I'll put you to bed."

Charley chuckled again. "Don't get excited, Frieda. What's there to get excited about? After all, it's a perfectly natural state of affairs. You can't get it from me, so you get it from someone else—"

"So?" Frieda shouted it. "Ain't that what you told me to do? You said it was all right if I—"

"Yes," Charley cut in softly.

"Then why the complaint? What are you complaining about?"

Charley didn't reply. He was chuckling again.

"Answer me," Frieda demanded. "Damn you, Charley—"

Charley stopped chuckling. He looked at Hart. He said, "You get the picture? You see what's happening here?"

"I don't see anything," Hart said.

"She really goes for you," Charley said. "You musta showed her a very nice time this afternoon. Musta given her something special."

Hart shrugged.

Charley said, "That's why she got burned up at Mattone when he advised you to take off. She'd be very upset if you took off."

Frieda stood up. She had her eyes aiming at empty air just about midway between Charley and Hart. She didn't say anything.

Charley went on talking as though Frieda was not in the room. "Maybe she's told you about me. About me and her, I mean. Like how it amounts to a problem because I'm jammed up somewhere inside and I can't do anything for her except on rare occasions. So there's no sense being a dog in the manger and I told her to get it from someone else. I think that was a nice gesture on my part. Don't you think so?"

Hart nodded.

"What I think," Charley went on, "it was a very nice gesture but the trouble is, every time I make these nice gestures I get taken for a ride. It never fails. It reminds me, one time I had a pet canary, really a dandy of a bird, I paid plenty for it. But the cage, it looks so stingy, not hardly big enough for the bird to fly around and get the proper exercise. So one day I open the cage and I figure she'll fly around the room and then come back and perch on my shoulder. And that's how I come to lose her. The window is open and out she goes."

It was quiet for some moments.

Then Charley looked at Frieda. And he said, "It ain't your fault, lady. I'm not blaming you."

Frieda remained standing. She went on staring at the empty space between Charley and Hart. She said, "He says it ain't my fault. He says—"

"I'm saying it's nobody's fault," Charley smiled. "If we gotta blame something, let's blame it on the climate. We got a weird climate here in Philadelphia."

Frieda closed her eyes. She put her hands to the sides of her head and her eyes stayed closed and she groaned.

"Yes," Charley murmured. "It hurts me, too. You got no idea how it hurts me."

Frieda opened her eyes. She looked at Charley. Her arms were lifted just a little, somewhat pleadingly. "Can't we—?"

"No," Charley said. "I wish we could, lady. But we can't. We just can't. If you wanted him just for a playmate I guess the three of us could manage it somehow, we could have an understanding. But it's more than having bedroom parties, you want him all the way, you got him so deep in your system you can feel him without touching him. So that chops it off between you and me."

"Complete?" Frieda's head was down.

"Clean break," Charley nodded. "We drop it, we forget about it, and you have my guarantee there won't be any grief."

"Charley—" She spoke thickly. "I wasn't looking for this to happen. I swear to you, Charley, it was—"

"The climate," Charley said. "We're always getting weather we don't expect."

In spades, Hart thought. He saw Charley getting up from the table, reaching for the bottle of gin, the bottle nestled gently in Charley's arm, pressed affectionately to Charley's chest. Then Charley was walking out of the room. For several moments nothing happened, and Hart sat there listening to Charley's footsteps moving off through the house and climbing up the stairs. When the sound of the footsteps was up there on the second floor, he heard other footsteps moving toward him. He looked up and saw Frieda approaching. She came in close and put her big beefy arms around him, sliding her fat rump onto his lap. She put her thick lips against his mouth.

Damn it, he said to himself. Damn it to hell.

ater that night Hart sat with Mattone and Rizzio, they were in the living room playing poker. Charley was upstairs in his room, out cold on the bed with the empty gin bottle clutched in both hands. They'd tried to free the bottle from his grip when he'd passed out, but it was as though his fingers were bolted to the glass and finally they ʒave it up. That was a couple hours ago, and now it was past eleven and the poker game had been in progress some ninety minutes. At this point the big winner was Mattone, with Rizzio a few dollars ahead and Hart's finances going down and down and getting close to nothing. Every now and then he'd get good cards but he couldn't do anything with them, he was distracted by sounds from upstairs where Frieda was hauling her belongings from one room to another. The sounds told him that Frieda was moving out of the room she shared with Myrna, taking her things into the room she would now share with him.

At half-past eleven Hart was down to three dollars and Mattone looked at the two bills and the silver and said, "You're nearly bankrupt."

"You want it?" Hart asked, pointing to the three dollars.

"Sure," Mattone grinned. "It's U.S. currency, ain't it?"

"Come on," Rizzio said to Mattone. "Deal the cards—"

"Wait," Hart murmured. He looked down at the three dollars. "Take it, Mattone. I'm giving it to you."

"No," Mattone said.

"Go on." He smiled at Mattone. "Take it."

"What is this?" Rizzio asked the two of them. "What goes on here?"

"He's offering me a gift," Mattone said.

Rizzio grimaced puzzledly. "I don't get it."

"I do," Mattone said.

"The hell you do," Hart told him. "You couldn't figure it if you had twice the brains you have."

"Listen, buddy." Mattone leaned forward just a little. "Do yourself a favor. Don't underestimate my brains."

"We gonna play poker?" Rizzio spoke impatiently.

"We're playing it now." Mattone was handling the deck, his fingers smooth on the cards, lightly shifting the cards from one hand to the other while he gazed intently at Hart's face. "I think this is bigger stakes than just cash."

"What in Christ's name goes on here?" Rizzio demanded.

"It's what they call bait," Mattone said to Rizzio. "He's tossing me a chunk of bait, that's all. If I nibble, he'll make it more. He'll wind up offering me a lot more than three dollars if I sign up with his team."

"What team?" Rizzio frowned.

"That team sitting there," Mattone said, pointing to Hart. "It's him and him and him. That's all he's got on his side. Just himself. He's looking for a team-mate."

"But—" Rizzio scratched the top of his head. "But that don't fit the picture. It ain't as if he's working alone. He's in with us, ain't he?"

Mattone pushed his eyebrows up. "Really?" he murmured, trying to be suave about it. "Where'd you get that flash?"

Rizzio shrugged stupidly. "Well, I just took it for granted—"

'The thing is," Mattone said, his voice like light oil, "never take anything for granted, Rizzio. Not in this house. Not when you're working for Charley."

"I thought—"

"That's another mistake you make," Mattone schooled him. "You always forget that Charley does all the thinking here."

Rizzio considered it for a moment, then nodded slowly and mumbled, "Maybe you're right."

"Of course I'm right," Mattone said. He leaned back comfortably and continued to pass the deck from one hand to the other. He'd reduced the grin to a thin smile and had it floating toward Hart, using it like a feather to tickle Hart's chin.

There was another noise from upstairs. It was a tiny noise, just a slight scraping of something against the floor and Mattone didn't hear it, Rizzio didn't hear it, but Hart heard it distinctly and acutely and he thought: She's moving things around in that room, putting this chair here and that chair there, and it's a cinch you'll soon be hearing the sound of the bedsprings when she tries the mattress. You're in for some heavy work with that Frieda and this afternoon was just a light session compared to what it's going to be from here on in. You're really in for it now, you'll be doing it and hating it. All right let's walk away from that; it isn't bedtime yet. You're sitting here facing Mattone, not Frieda, and he's under the impression the only thing you got on your chest is him and his oily smile, his smooth talk that tries so hard to slide under your skin. He'd jump for joy if you'd start sweating and cracking up. I think if you let him take it far enough he could really get on your nerves. He's certainly a skunk and although the only way to deal with skunks is keep far away from them it stands to reason you can't put distance between yourself and this one here, so what's to do except get up there on the mound and pitch a few at his head. We'll see if we can get that smile off his face.

He heard Mattone saying, "You look lonesome, mister. I never seen anyone look so lonesome."

"It isn't that," he said. He looked down at the three dollars. "I was wondering about this," indicating the money. "Just trying to remember why I offered it to you."

"But I told you why," with the light oil dripping again, the smile ever so soft and thin. "You want me on your team."

Hart pretended a thoughtful frown. He spoke absently. "No, I don't think so. It couldn't be for that reason."

"Wanna bet?" And Mattone flicked a wink at Rizzio.

"What I think is—" Hart held onto the thoughtful frown,

his voice vague as he imitated someone talking aloud to himself, "—maybe there was no reason at all."

"You can't fool me," Mattone sneered. "I ain't no imbecile like this one here," pointing to Rizzio. The pointing finger moved so that it aimed at the three dollars. "Three worms on the hook, that's what it is. You're lonesome and you want company. You're scared and you want help."

"That would make sense," Hart said, still frowning thoughtfully, "except for a list of items we maybe ought to look at."

"All right," Mattone said. He tried to put a sneer in it. "Let's take a look."

"First thing," Hart said, "the girl. What's her name again?"

"Myrna. Her name is Myrna." And Mattone glanced sideways at his injured arm.

"Well, what I'm saying is," Hart said, "that's item one and we can cross it off; the girl doesn't scare me."

"You sure?" Mattone prodded.

Hart shrugged. He tossed it away with, "She tries anything, I'll clip her in the teeth."

Mattone was trying to be suave again, the oil coming back to his voice as he said, "That's a privilege reserved side. This ain't no social club where all you gotta do is pay a fee to join up. This is what they call a very tight outfit, and as far as you're concerned I'm willing to bet—"

"Save your money," Hart spoke softly. And then he pitched it, "I get the wire from Charley I'm working Friday night."

"Friday—" Mattone blinked a few times. "Charley told you about Friday night?"

This is fun, Hart said to himself. He was nodding slowly, saying, "The Kenniston place."

Mattone looked at Rizzio and said, "You hear this?"

"So?" Rizzio made a meaningless gesture. "So I hear it. So what?"

Mattone had his mouth open but he couldn't talk.

Hart said, "That crosses off item two. I think it sorta louses up your theory that I'm scared. Don't you think so?"

There was no answer, not in words, anyway. Mattone made a straining effort to say something, but all that came out was a twisted grunt.

76

"Another thing you said," Hart went on, "you made the claim I'm lonesome and I want company. And that brings up item three. It's a little favor Charley did for me tonight, the kind of favor he wouldn't do if I was on the outside or even halfway in, or let's say ninety-nine percent in. He did something an Eskimo husband does when you're his guest, except the Eskimo gives her to you for only one night, and Charley's letting me have her on a permanent basis. He's—"

It didn't need more than that. Mattone had leaped up and the deck of cards was out of his hand, the cards flying off the table.

"You're—" Mattone wrestled with it, choked on it. "You've done it, haven't you? You've really moved in."

Hart didn't reply. He sat there looking at the dismay and defeat in Mattone's eyes. He wondered what showed in his own eyes. Whatever it was, it had nothing to do with contentment. He told himself he mustn't let it show, and he tried to get it out of his eyes but before he could do that he heard a squeak from the mattress upstairs.

And he heard Mattone saying, "You don't seem happy about it."

He shrugged. So here it is, he said to himself. It shows and you know it shows, there comes a time when you just can't pretend.

The truth of it sent a slight quiver along his spine. Mattone was correct after all, you're scared and you're lonesome, there's no one on your team but you and you and you. It's a kind of starvation, and it isn't easy to take, that's for sure. Damn sure.

But later of course it was pretending again when in the bed with Frieda. Somehow it was easier than it had been in the afternoon, but that was due to the darkness of the room, in the afternoon the daylight factor had handicapped him because every now and then she wanted him to look at her. Now in the dark she couldn't ask him to do that, except at one point she murmured maybe they ought to switch on the lamp. He didn't say anything, but kept her too busy to execute the idea.

The sighs that came from his lips were sheer pleasure. But if she'd switched on the lamp and seen the look on his face it would have gone bad, because the look on his face was the tight-wrinkled grimace of doing something extremely unpleasant. There was no way to rub off the grimace; it would stay there just as long as the ordeal went on, the hammering ordeal of feeling the insistency of her fat arms around him, her gasping and moaning that was inexhaustible. From time to time he'd wonder what the clock showed. Its illuminated face was on the table across the room but he couldn't even turn his head to look, she was holding him too tightly.

Yet all at once she loosened her hold and mumbled, "Cigarette," and he rolled away from her, an almost frenzied motion like a fish rolling out of a loosened net. The cigarettes and matches were on the floor and as he reached down blindly he almost fell off the bed.

He heard her saying, "Whatsa matter? You tired."

"Me?" He held back a crazy laugh. "I haven't even started yet."

She took him seriously. She said, "I knew it the first time I put eyes on you."

He handed her a lit cigarette, took a long puff from his own. He was resting flat on his back and gazing across the room at the clock whose green numbers showed twenty minutes past three.

"Tell me something," she said.

"Like what?"

"Anything," she said. "Just talk to me."

"All right." He thought for a moment. And then, not too sure of where it would go, "Ever hear of Indianapolis?"

"Where they teach the sailors?"

"No," he said. "Not Annapolis. Indianapolis."

"So?"

"It's where they have the big race. The auto race."

"On the fourth of July?"

"Memorial Day."

"That's what I said. The fourth of July?" She sounded

rather sleepy. Or maybe it was because she had no interest in the topic.

He said, "It's May thirtieth. You're getting your holidays mixed up."

"What?" And then, more distinctly, "What the hell are we talking about?"

"Indianapolis," he said. "The five-hundred-mile race on Memorial Day."

"You were in it?" Sleepily again. "You a racing car driver?"

"No," he said, "just a spectator. I guess you'd call me a fan. This thing at Indianapolis is something to see and every chance I had I'd go there. I remember one year I was lucky and made friends with some mechanics, and they let me hang around the pits. The pits are where the cars come in for fuel and repairs. It's all very interesting, the way they change a tire in thirty seconds, and when it's the engine they jump right into it and it's fixed in no time at all. And they—"

"All right, all right. What's the point?"

As though she hadn't spoken, he went on, "—they cater to that car as though it's something alive. It's a very expensive piece of engineering, and when you look at the motor, you know it's something out of the ordinary. You know that's stamina there, that's real stamina, it'll never wear out."

She blew some smoke out of her mouth. She didn't say anything.

Hart said, "What happens, though, some drivers are too anxious and they forget the race is for five hundred miles, they force it too much, and after a hundred laps or so it can't take the strain and there's a breakdown. Sometimes it's a serious breakdown, the kind they can't fix in the pits. So then the car is out of the race, and it's a pity, really. You see the driver biting his lip to keep from crying like a baby. But of course he has no one to blame but himself."

She remained quiet for some moments. And then, her voice low but not at all sleepy, "You making stipulations?"

"Not exactly."

"Come on, come on." She sat up, looking down at him in the darkness. "Let's not play party games. You wanna tell me something, come on and tell me."

"Well—" and he paused for a timing effect, "I don't want to spoil anything—"

"Be careful, mister." It was a definite warning, as though she had a can of lye in her hand. "Be very careful."

"I'll try my best," he said.

"Is that for a laugh? If it is, I'm not laughing."

"Look—" and again he timed it, used the tiny interval of quiet to drag at his cigarette. "Whaddya say we drop it?"

"No." She sat up straighter. "This deal is for keeps and we're gonna settle all issues right at the beginning."

"For keeps," he murmured thoughtfully. "That's a lot longer than five hundred miles."

"You'll last it out," she said. "I'm not worried about that."

"It's more than just that," he said. "On my side everything checks, I know exactly where I stand. But you sound as though you're not sure—"

"Me?" Her voice was harsh with a sort of fishwife intimacy. "Did I bring up this thing about Annapolis?"

"I'll tell you, Frieda," he said conversationally. "It's your driving technique I'm getting at. It started me to thinking about that racing car. About the way it breaks down when you push it too fast. Or maybe—you're doing it deliberately."

"Doing what?"

"Getting all you can while the getting is good."

"Whadda ya mean? You mean I'm worried you'll change your mind?"

"No, that isn't what I mean."

"Then what the hell do you mean?"

"I mean, maybe you're worried about yourself. That maybe you'll change your own mind."

"And toss you overboard?"

"That's one way of putting it."

"But why would I do that?" Her voice lowered just a trifle, there was a trace of uncertainty in her tone. "Why would I give you up when I know you fill the bill completely, when I got what I been looking for, all them months and months of waiting, and then it comes along and I get it, so now I have it and why should I give it up?"

"I can't tell you. I'm waiting for you to tell me."

"Now look," she said, "this talk is getting on my nerves."

"All right. Let's go to sleep."

There was an ashtray on the floor and he took the stubs of their cigarettes and mashed them in the tray. Then, settling himself on his side, he worked his head comfortably into the pillow. Frieda remained sitting up, staring into the dark. After a while, she was reaching over the side of the bed, going for the cigarettes and the matches and the ashtray.

Hart was drifting into sleep and going down and getting the good cloudy feeling that comes just before the slumber takes hold, and then he heard the noise of a match against a matchbook. He smiled dimly and thought, There's nothing like tobacco to steady the nerves.

And a little while later he heard it again, match against matchbook. His eyes were open now because he wanted to stay awake, he liked this noise she was making striking matches. Now there was a lot of smoke around the head of the bed and he inhaled it, sensed the thickness of it and knew she was taking long, thirsty drags.

He was counting it off each time she struck a match, and now she was on the fifth cigarette. He said to himself: Let's figure seven or eight minutes for each cigarette; that makes it around forty minutes she's been sitting there with her problem, the way she's eating up that smoke she's nowhere near getting it solved, or maybe she has it solved already and she doesn't like what came out in the answer. One thing for sure, it's no fun for her. I'll tell you something here, it begins to look as though Charley was right when he said she really went for you, went a long ways deeper than just wanting you for this horizontal business, I'm ready to think she's got what they call the real feeling, and that's bad no that's good no that's bad, oh make up your mind, for Christ's sake, get your strategy straight, will you? This is a fine time to take your hands off the wheel, like on the north turn at Indianapolis—and what got you started with Indianapolis, anyway? You fell right into trouble with that one. And tried to climb out and fell in deeper when you put the problem in her lap, putting a smile on your face when you thought you had her backed up in a corner, when all the time it's you who's pressed against the wall, it oughta be you sitting up and chewing on cigarettes, and there she goes lighting up number six—

A few moments later her hand was on his shoulder.

"You sleeping?" she asked.

He didn't answer.

"Wake up," she said. She shook him.

He imitated a yawn. "What time is it?"

"Come on, wake up. We're getting dressed."

"What?" He frowned, his eyes aiming across to the clock that stated ten minutes past four. He said, "Are you kidding? It's still dark outside."

"That's good," she said. "That's perfect."

He sat up slowly. He stared at her. She was dragging at the cigarette and the glow of the burning end was intensified, he could see the expression on her face and it was somewhere between calm and frantic purpose.

She said, "Let's hurry and get dressed. We're checking out of here."

She switched on the lamp and started to climb out of bed but he took hold of her wrist and said quietly, "Wait, now. Let's talk this over—"

"We'll talk later." She made an impatient grimace and tried to pull her wrist free.

But he held on. "I'd rather talk about it now. Before I do a thing, I like to know why I'm doing it."

She closed her eyes. She took a deep breath. "Please," she murmured, "don't make it tougher on me. It's tough enough as it is."

He let go of her wrist. "It needs discussion, Frieda." He gave her a smile to let her know she wasn't alone with her trouble. And then, edging closer to her, placing his hand on her shoulder, "What is it? What's this talk about checking out?"

"We gotta do it, that's all."

"But why?"

"Because," she said, "I'm afraid."

"Charley?"

"No," she said. "Not Charley." She sat there gazing

straight ahead. "I'm afraid of myself. Of what I'm liable
to do—"

"To me?"

"To both of us." And now she looked at him. "It's something I was trying not to think about. I almost managed to
get it out of my head. But then you started with that talk
about the racing cars. With me the driver and you the
engine. Like telling me I'm covering all the ground I can
right now because I'm not sure about later. Not sure of
myself, I mean."

He didn't say anything.

Frieda said, "What I'm saying is, I just don't trust myself.
I'm afraid I might open my mouth."

He stiffened slightly.

And then he heard her saying, "It's this New Orleans
business. The story you told Charley. You said the reason
you killed your brother was money. But the point is, you
didn't do it for money."

The stiffness increased and it was like the cold steel of a
forceps taking hold and tightening.

"I know you didn't do it for money," she said. "I don't
know why you did it, but I'm sure of one thing, it wasn't
financial. I found that out today when we were in the
kitchen and the talk got around to New Orleans and your
brother—" she took a deep breath, "—I was watching the
look on your face."

His hand reached for the cigarettes. His other hand
went for the matches. He had to do something with his
hands.

"And there it is, there's our trouble," she said. "You
didn't do it for cash and so you're not a professional. And
you know what happens if Charley finds out you're not a
professional."

He was trying to light the cigarette but for some reason
the smoke wouldn't pull.

"We gotta get out of this house," Frieda said. "We gotta
get out before I spill it to Charley."

The match went out. He lit another and got the cigarette
lit. He said, "I don't believe you'd do that."

"Wouldn't I? You forget something. I'm on Charley's
payroll."

He frowned. "Let's try it again. That one went over my head."

"All right, we'll put it this way—I've been in this game a long time. I've developed certain habits, certain things I do without thinking—like a machine goes into action when the man pulls the lever. So maybe Charley asks a question and I answer it—"

He was shaking his head, giving her a smile of kindly contradiction. "I can't go along with that. You're stretching the point."

"There's another point." Her voice lowered and thickened. "I'm a woman."

And she paused to let it sink in.

And then she said, "It adds up something like this—when a woman really goes for a man, there's a thing happens inside her, I can't explain exactly what it is, it's sort of on the crazy side, a woman gets in that condition she ain't really responsible for what she's prone to do."

"Now look," he tried a little laugh, "it can't be that bad."

"It can't?" She returned the laugh, giving it a tight twist that made it almost a groan. "If only I could make it plain to you, what happens to us females when we get that one-man feeling. You look at me close enough, you'll see it's a kind of sickness."

"Like what?"

"I don't know. All I know is, you got me dizzy. You got me delirious. I'm so goddam hungry for you—" It was too thick for her throat and she choked on it. And then, catching her breath, trying to get in stride again, "The thing we need the most, it's got to be there all the time, and if I get to thinking it ain't there, I'll flip my lid, I really will."

He said aloud to himself, "This lady ain't kidding."

"I'm so glad you know it." And she gazed at him with a mixture of petal-soft tenderness and rock-hard warning, the warning saying: Just watch your step, mister, you make the slightest move to pull away from me and I'll whisper something in Charley's ear. But in the next instant the warning melted away and there was only the tenderness. Again she took hold of his arms. She said, "Let's play it safe so it won't ever happen. We'll get away from here, away from Charley, away from all of them. It'll be just you and me, we'll get on a train going somewhere—"

"No," he said.

"Why not?" Her fingers tightened on his arm. "What's to stop us?"

"Law." And he shrugged. "You know the way it is. I can't do any traveling right now. There's too many eyes looking for me."

"We'll get past them. We'll figure some way."

He shook his head. "It can't be done, Frieda. They got me traced here to Philly. Stands to reason they have men at every train station and bus depot."

"The waterfront," as she snapped her fingers. "I got some friends along the waterfront."

"That sounds convenient. Only trouble is, in a case like this the Law is very waterfront-conscious. They'll be watching each and every pier."

She laughed sourly. "I oughta be highly pleased. I'm in bed with a celebrity."

"Yes, I'm in great demand these days."

"Tell me about New Orleans. Why did you kill your brother?"

He shrugged.

"Come on," she said. "Tell me."

He shrugged again.

"Why won't you tell me?"

He spoke aloud to himself. "We're past that part of the program."

"In other words, you just can't talk about it and you wish I'd lay off?"

"Something like that." He wasn't looking at her.

He heard her saying, "Hey, mister, I'm still here. Don't hang up on me."

"I'm listening."

"Come closer, you'll hear better."

He moved closer to her so that their thighs touched but he didn't feel the contact, he didn't feel anything at all or see anything in this room. He was thinking about New Orleans.

Frieda put her arm around his middle. Her fingers played along his ribs. She said, "Well anyway, I guess you're right about the Law. It adds up we can't leave this house, we're stuck here."

He made an acute straining effort and managed to pull himself away from New Orleans. He looked at Frieda and made a fatalistic gesture, saying, "Gotta take things as they come."

"Yeah," she admitted. "No use losing sleep about it."

He grinned at her. "That's the way to talk."

"Sure," she said. "Nobody knows what's gonna happen. So what's the use of worrying? Only thing to do is have our fun while we're here."

"Correct," he said. "Keep it up. You're doing fine."

"Yeah, I'm really in form?" But then her eyes were shut tightly and her hand fell away from his side and she said aloud to herself, "If only I was able to convince myself, to get myself to believe it's just for fun—if only I didn't go for him so much, this bastard here—"

"Now look," he cut in gently. "Don't start that again."

"Listen—that noise—downstairs."

"I don't hear anything."

"Listen," she said. "Listen to it."

And then he heard it, a muffled cry, then a chair getting knocked over? And now another cry.

He was out of bed and reaching for his trousers.

"No," Frieda said. "You stay out of it."

From downstairs there was Mattone's voice cursing and saying, "You want more? I'll give you more—" And then a thud and a crash and Myrna shrieking again.

"I tell you no," Frieda said loudly. "Come back here."

Hart ran out of the room.

He was halfway down the stairs when he saw them in the living room, Myrna sitting on the floor with her face in her hands, Mattone in his pajamas standing over her, his mouth tight and vindictive, a suggestion of enjoyment in his eyes. There were two chairs knocked over, and a lamp. And on the sofa, also wearing pajamas,

Rizzio sat holding his hand to the side of his face.

Hart took in all of that, wondered about it for a moment, then saw the opened suitcase near the vestibule. Some of the contents had spilled out and he saw a skirt and a brassiere and a high-heeled shoe. He was moving slowly now as he descended the rest of the stairs.

Mattone looked up and saw him. Mattone said, "Go back to bed. We don't need you."

"What happened?" Hart asked mildly.

Rizzio took his hand away from his face that showed some fingernail scratches. "She's crazy, this girl," Rizzio said. "She's gotta be loony to think she can pull a caper like this."

Myrna was trying to get to her feet. She almost made it, then fell on her side and stayed there for some moments. Then she tried again and this time she made it. Hart saw a thin stream of red going down from the corner of her mouth. She stood motionless, gazing at the opened suitcase. She took a step toward the suitcase and Mattone took hold of her arm.

"You want some more?" Mattone asked.

"Let go," she said dully. "I'm getting outta here."

"She's really gone crazy," Rizzio said. "We better wake up Charley."

"This don't require Charley," Mattone said. "I know just how to handle it."

Myrna tried to squirm away from Mattone's grip. He twisted her arm behind her back and she went to her knees. Her face was very white but there was no expression on it. And Hart wondered why she wasn't weeping. Mattone was really hurting her. She looked awfully frail and helpless kneeling there at Mattone's feet.

"What we oughta do," Rizzio said, "is get a rope and tie her up."

"No," Mattone said. "We won't hafta do that."

"Well, we gotta do something," Rizzio whined. "I wanna get this over with and go back to sleep."

Myrna squirmed again and Mattone put more pressure on her arm. Now he had her arm pulled up high between her shoulder blades and her head was down very low.

"I think she's coming around," Mattone murmured. "She

knows she made a mistake and she won't try it again."

"You sure of that?" Hart asked.

"Positive." Mattone looked at Hart. "She's finished for the night. She won't gimme any more trouble."

"Then why don't you let go of her arm?"

"Who's asking you?"

Hart shrugged. "No use breaking her arm."

"Suppose I wanna break it?"

Hart shrugged again. "No use talking that way, either."

"That's only your opinion," Mattone said. "If I feel like doing it, I'll break her neck."

"No you won't," Hart said. He was beginning to realize why he'd come running downstairs.

Mattone said, "Do yourself a favor, jimmy-boy. Don't agitate me. I been agitated enough tonight and I can take only so much."

"All right," Hart said. "That sounds reasonable. But you're hurting her and I think you oughta let go of her arm."

"The hell with what you think." Mattone looked away from Hart and looked down at Myrna who'd stopped squirming and was altogether passive under the pressure of his grip. He did nothing for a moment, and then he took in a hissing breath between his teeth and yanked viciously at her arm. She let out a screech of animal pain and Hart heard it going into him like a hook, the hook in there deep and pulling him forward toward Mattone. His right hand was a fist going up and over and down and hitting Mattone on the temple. Mattone let go of Myrna and staggered sideways, then straightened and grinned. Mattone said, "Know something? I was hoping you'd do that."

Hart grinned back at the tall good-looking light-heavyweight who now raised his arms very slowly, getting set with the right held high, the left easing out tentatively to either feint or lead, the legs arranged in a purely professional stance. Then Mattone began to move in.

Rizzio jumped up from the sofa, saying, "Aw, no, for Christ's sake. No—" and he snatched at the fabric of Mattone's pajama-shirt. But then he took Mattone's backward-jabbing elbow in his chest that sent him back to the sofa and he sat down, looking very worried.

Mattone resumed moving in, coming in slowly.

Hart backed away, then shifted off to one side, looking for a vase or a heavy ashtray or anything at all that might come in handy. He heard Mattone saying, "I could do it with one punch but I ain't gonna do it that way." And there was no vase or ashtray in the immediate vicinity, there was nothing except Mattone's left hand shooting out and almost getting him. He'd moved his head to pull away from it and now his hands were up defensively, the grin was off his face and his eyes became technical, not blinking as he heard Mattone murmuring, "What we're gonna do first, jimmy-boy, is some dental work. You got too many front teeth." So then the left jabbed again, jabbed very fast and neatly but he was ready for it and wiped it off with his right hand coming down as he moved in low and hooked his left to Mattone's middle. "Oh," Mattone said, but it wasn't a grunt, just a slight show of surprise, "that was sorta cute. This looks to be a cutey here. I always like it with these cuties, it's a lotta fun."

So then Mattone moved in again and Hart was cute once more, starting to the left, then to the right, then to the left again to avoid a series of jabs and a chopping right aimed at his jaw. But then Mattone found him with a short left hook to the middle and he took the full force of it, started to bend double, took a right to the side of his head, then another hook to the ribs, and knew he didn't have a chance and was due to get badly hurt. He managed to slip away from a whizzing left coming toward his eyes, ducked very low under another hook trying for his head, stabbed his own left into Mattone's stomach, then received a swinging right that crashed against the side of his skull and put some flashing vari-colored lights in there. He thought: The difficulty is, there's not enough room to move around, it's so much smaller than a regulation ring. He was grinning again, sending the grin past Mattone and giving it to Rizzio who sat there on the sofa shaking his head sadly, then giving it to Myrna who remained kneeling on the floor, rubbing her arm. Then he heard footsteps on the stairs and Frieda's voice yelling they should stop it, while the bright green and orange and lavender lights in his head began to spin rapidly, impelled by Mattone's right hand getting him on the forehead. He told himself he might as well fall down, but as he went down he knew that wouldn't stop Mattone from continuing with him while he was on the floor, and he tried to get up, grabbing at Mattone's middle for support. Mattone pushed him away, set him up with a light jab to the chest, and hauled off with the right, not aiming it for the jaw, but preparing it for damage to the eyes. And Hart saw it coming, and thought in that instant: He'll close both of my eyes, then work on my nose, then my mouth and he won't put across that finishing touch until he's got my face completely ruined. But for some reason the blow didn't land. He was only semi-conscious now, and he wondered vaguely why Mattone had stopped the punch when it was more than halfway home. He blinked hard several times and saw Mattone moving away, Mattone's face in profile. So of course he knew what it had to be, and he looked toward the stairway and saw Charley standing there on the steps above Frieda. Some yellow light came down from the hall upstairs and fell softly on the shiny fabric of Charley's bathrobe. Charley had one hand in a pocket of the robe and in the other hand he held a gun.

The gun wasn't aimed at anything in particular. Somehow it didn't seem like a weapon in Charley's hand, more on the order of a briar-pipe he was holding just to hold onto something. Under his eyes there was the purple of hangover. But aside from that, he didn't seem sick or sloppy or weary. He looked completely awake and quietly capable.

Mattone said, "Now look, Charley—"

"Hold it," Charley said, not looking at Mattone. He came down the stairs past Frieda, then across the carpet past Mattone. He seated himself on the sofa beside Rizzio and then, his head turning slowly, he examined the room with its overturned chairs, its wrinkled carpet, the girl kneeling on the floor near the opened suitcase, and Mattone who stood facing him, breathing hard through the nose. He didn't look at Hart.

Mattone said, "I'll tell it, Charley. Let me tell it—"

"You be quiet," Charley said. "I've had enough from you, Mattone. You open your mouth again and I'll shoot you in the kneecap."

On the stairs, Frieda said quickly, "He means it, Mattone. For God's sake, keep your mouth shut."

Charley looked at Rizzio and murmured, "Give it to me."

"Well," Rizzio said, "I'm sound asleep and Mattone wakes me up and says he hears something downstairs. So then he runs downstairs and I follow him and I see him going after Myrna. She's got that suitcase in her hand and so I know it ain't for no stroll around the block. He grabs her and she pulls away and then I grab her and she does this to my face. So he grabs her again and she won't behave, he's gotta mess her up a little to quiet her down. Then Al tells him to leave her alone and it gets to be an argument and—" Rizzio shrugged.

Charley put the gun in the pocket of his bathrobe. He ran a forefinger slowly across his underlip. His head turned very slowly toward Myrna and he said, "Get up from the floor."

Myrna didn't move.

"It's in the head," Rizzio said. "This girl here is sick in the head."

"Get her a drink," Charley said.

"No," Myrna said. "I don't need a drink."

"What's the matter with you?" Charley asked.

"Nothing," she answered. "I just wanna leave, that's all."

"You can't do that," Charley said very softly. "You know we can't let you do that."

"Yes," she said. There was nothing in her voice, nothing at all. "I know how it is, Charley. I shouldn't of done it. I won't try it again."

"I hope you won't," Charley had it down to a whisper.

"The hell she won't," Mattone said.

Charley's eyes were closed. "I'm begging you, Mattone. I'm actually begging you to keep quiet. You don't know how close you came to getting shot."

Mattone's mouth slackened, then tightened, and slackened again. His eyes became wet. He tried to hold back the wetness but it came out and rolled down his cheeks. He said, "Always blaming me. Why is it me all the time?"

"You're a louse-up artist, that's why," Charley told him. "You're always lousing up a situation. I've tried to tell you how things should be handled, but you never listen."

"I did what I thought was—"

"Not what you thought was practical, don't tell me that. You got no idea what it is to be practical. With you it's muscle, always muscle. The mistake you made, you never should have quit the ring. That's all you're good for, demonstrating your muscle."

Mattone stood there making no sound as the tears came out of his eyes.

"I'll let you demonstrate it now," Charley said. "Come on, use some muscle and pick up the chairs. Straighten up this room."

"Charley, you can't treat me like a—"

"Yes I can," Charley said. He gestured toward the overturned chairs. "Pick them up."

Mattone wouldn't or couldn't move, and Frieda came quickly down the stairs, saying, "I'll do it—"

"No," Charley said. "He'll do it."

"Will I?" Mattone's voice broke.

"Yes, you will," Charley said, then looked away from Mattone as though to say the subject was dropped. Mattone moved toward the overturned chairs. For some moments it was quiet in the room except for the sound of Mattone setting the chairs on their legs, then straightening the carpet. Rizzio stretched and yawned and said sleepily, "You want me for anything, Charley?" And Charley shook his head. Rizzio yawned again and got up from the sofa, crossed the room and went upstairs. Frieda said to Hart, "All right, it's all over. Let's go back to bed." Charley said, "No, Frieda. I want him down here. I wanna talk to him." Frieda said, "Me too?" And Charley murmured, "No, you go up and get some sleep. He'll be up soon." And then, to Mattone, "All right, that's enough with the carpet." Mattone, not looking at him, spoke with bitter sarcasm. "You want me to wash the floor?"

"No," Charley said. "Just wash your face. Go up and wash your face and go to bed."

Mattone followed Frieda upstairs. Myrna had lifted herself from the floor and now she was slowly re-filling her suitcase. When she had it filled, she carried it toward the stairway but Charley stopped her with, "Not yet, Myrna. Sit down for a while."

She lowered the suitcase to the stairway landing. She came over to the sofa and sat down beside Charley.

Hart took one of the armchairs. He felt chilly wearing only his trousers. He told himself it was awfully cold down here. He wished he had something to cover his chest and shoulders, and trying to concentrate on that, he heard himself saying, "I can tell you what it is, Charley. She did it on account of me."

"Let her tell it," Charley said.

Myrna didn't say anything.

Charley looked at her. "I'm trying to help you, kid. I wanna do everything I can to help you."

She sat there looking at the carpet. She was like a lost child sitting in some station-house, no hope in her eyes.

Charley put his hand on her shoulder. "I can't help you if you don't talk. You gotta talk. You gotta get it out."

"I can't," she said.

"Give it a try," Charley urged gently.

She sighed heavily. Then she tried to speak and she couldn't speak.

Charley said, "You got me plenty worried, kid."

"I know." Her head was down. "I'm sorry, Charley. I'm so sorry—"

"This walking-out business. I'm worried you'll try it again. And maybe next time you'll make it. So then they pick you up—"

"For what? I'm not on the wanted list."

"You think you're not. You forget all them times they hauled you in on suspicion. So all right, the way it was then you knew just what to say and how to say it. But now it's different, you got yourself all knotted up inside, you're in no shape to handle their questions. And before you know it you're breaking down and spilling everything."

"I wouldn't do that, Charley. I'd never do a thing like that to you."

"Not in your right mind you wouldn't. But the way it is now, you got no grip on yourself. You're a long way off from anywhere."

She gazed across the room at the packed suitcase.

For some moments it was quiet. Then Charley said very softly, "You see the way it is, kid? I can't take any chances.

If you don't snap out of it, I'll hafta get rid of you."

"You mean—I'm gonna die?"

Charley took his hand off her shoulder. He didn't say anything.

"Yes," she said, "you're telling me I'm gonna die. And then you hafta do away with the body. So it goes where my brother went. It goes down the cellar and into the furnace."

And Hart thought: This is actually happening, look at Charley's face, look at him there getting up from the sofa and taking the gun out of his pocket. And look at her, Jesus Christ, look at her, she isn't even blinking.

"Well, kid?" Charley's voice was purely technical. "What's it gonna be?"

She smiled at Charley. "All I can say is, thanks for everything. You did a lot for me, Charley. You were awfully good to me and Paul."

Charley stood a few feet away from her. He had the gun aimed at her head. She went on smiling, sitting there not moving. Hart could feel the coldness of the room and now it had nothing to do with the weather outside. The coldness came from the ice in Charley's brain. Because Charley was completely a professional and therefore functioning according to the rigid doctrine of the outlaw code. So the only thing the gun was pointed at was an obstacle that had to be removed.

Hart heard himself saying, "Hold it, Charley."

"No," Charley said. "I tried to pull her out of it and I couldn't. So she's done. Can't you see she's done?"

"Not yet," Hart said. He got up from the chair. He did it slowly but with enough noise to delay the action of Charley's finger on the trigger.

"What's the matter?" Charley asked him, not looking at him. "What are you doing?"

"Nothing special," Hart said. "I'm just thinking there's another way to do it."

"How you mean?" Charley spoke to him as one professional to another. "You mean with a knife or something?"

"I meant there's another way to bring her around," Hart said.

Charley looked at him.

And Hart said, "Put the gun in her hand."

Charley winced slightly. Then he frowned.

Hart looked at Myrna. "Tell him you want the gun. Tell him you want to shoot me."

Myrna closed her eyes. She shivered.

"You get it?" Hart said to Charley. "She tries to walk out of this house to get away from me. This man here who killed Paul. She says to herself, if she stays here she'll find some way to murder me. She doesn't want to murder me. And yet she does. She's on a see-saw. Only way to get her off it is hand her the gun, let her make up her mind here and now."

Charley went on frowning at him. "Maybe you think this gun ain't loaded?"

"I know it's loaded."

"And you're really willing to take the chance?"

Hart nodded.

"You're quite a gambler," Charley said.

"Not a smart one. Just curious. I'm very curious now."

Charley grinned stiffly. "What's that they say about the cat?"

"Yes, it got the cat, all right."

"Well," Charley said, and he wasn't grinning now, "there's one nice thing about this. It lets me out."

Hart saw the gun twirling on Charley's finger in the trigger guard, the barrel coming into Charley's grasp, the butt extended toward Myrna. She shivered again, then reached out and took the gun from Charley. She looked at it, got a trembling grip on it, and aimed it at Hart.

He stood there waiting for it to hit him. It would be a .38 slug going into him high in the chest or possibly the throat. Her eyes were focused on that area and he told himself the look on her face was entirely clinical, as though the only thought in her brain was to put the bullet where it would finish him. Then he tried to tell himself he was mistaken about that, maybe she wasn't seeing him at all, maybe she was seeing inside herself and trying to get things cleared up in there. Well, whichever way it was going, he wished she'd hurry up and settle it. He hadn't expected the waiting would be this difficult. But he wasn't sorry he'd told Charley to hand her the gun.

It isn't exactly suicide, he thought. It's more on the order of sacrifice. Some of us are sacrifice-prone instead of accident-prone, we see something and it grows on us, we come to adore it, and all at once we hear the mandolins and get the picture of that moonlight pouring through the trees. It has no connection with logic or anything you can put your finger on, it's just got to be classified as mystical. You're making this sacrifice for purely mystical reasons. If she wants you dead you're willing to be dead. And another thing you know, this waiting is difficult only because you feel the pain she's having, like a current going through a wire from her to you. Look at her eyes, oh Jesus Christ look what's in her eyes.

She lowered the gun.

"No deal?" Charley murmured.

She didn't answer. The gun rested in her lap. Charley reached out and took it. For a few moments he stood close to her, studying her face. Then he put the gun in his bathrobe pocket and looked at Hart and said, "I think she's all right now."

"Of course she's all right."

She was smiling at Hart. It was a dim smile. She said, "You know what I'm thinking?"

"Yes," Hart said. "I know."

"She's thanking you," Charley said. "She feels a lot better now and she's saying thanks."

Without sound Hart said to Charley: You don't know the half of it, not even a small part of it.

"She's gonna like you now," Charley said. "You and her are gonna be friends. Ain't that right, Myrna?"

She nodded slowly, but it wasn't a reply to Charley's query. It was in agreement with something she was saying to herself.

Charley said, "Well, I guess what we oughta do now is get some sleep."

"I'm not sleepy," Hart said.

"Me neither," Myrna murmured. "I'd like to sit here for a while and talk."

"To him?" Charley asked.

"Yes," she said. "That is, if it's all right with you, Charley."

"I think it's a swell idea," Charley smiled. "You and him'll have a nice talk and get to be good friends."

"Would you do me a favor, Charley?"

"Sure, Myrna. Anything."

"Would you carry my suitcase upstairs?"

"It'll be a pleasure," Charley said. He turned and went to the stairway and picked up the suitcase. He started up the stairs, then stopped and looked at Hart. "You better put something on. There's no heat in this house, I don't want you catching cold."

"I'm all right," Hart said.

"I want you to stay in shape. You're a valuable piece of property."

"Mattone doesn't think so."

"Mattone don't think, period." Charley smiled. "Don't you worry about Mattone. Don't you worry about anything now. You're doing fine in this league."

"Thanks, Charley. But you didn't need to say it. I wasn't worrying."

"Not much you weren't," Charley chuckled. "You were jam-packed with worry." He patted his hand against the gun in his pocket. "This tool here had you scared sick. But you covered it up. I sure like the way you covered it up."

And Hart thought, So maybe Frieda was wrong, after all. This man is only a human being and he can be fooled. Aloud he said, "Tell Frieda I'll be up soon."

"All right," Charley said. "But don't keep her waiting too long."

"I won't."

Charley smiled complacently at both of them. Then he continued up the stairs and they heard his footsteps on the second floor, the bedroom door opening and closing. Hart listened for more sounds from upstairs but there were none and he could feel the quiet cold and dead up there and sweet-cool down here, really a fine climate down here in the living room so very far away from upstairs.

He went to the sofa and sat beside her, not touching her but feeling something so much deeper than touching. He looked at her, his eyes telling her, and he said, "You see how it is?"

"Yes," she said. "But how did it happen?"

"It just happened."

"I could feel it happening. I knew and you knew, we both knew."

"It's sorta funny," he said.

"But not to laugh about."

"Certainly not. It isn't that kind of comedy."

"What you mean is, it's funny the way it happened, but now that it's happened it's serious."

"That's exactly what I mean," he said. "It's very serious."

"What are we gonna do?"

"I don't know. You got any ideas?"

She shook her head.

"Well," he murmured, "let's try to think."

"I can't," she said. "I can't get any thoughts now."

"Neither can I. And that's the hell of it."

"Tell me something," she said. "Has this ever happened to you before?"

"No."

"Same here," she said.

"It's like—"

"Like—"

"We just can't say what it's like," he told her. "There's no way to say it."

"Maybe it's like when you're walking along and all at once you get hit by lightning."

"No," he said. "That would be negative. There's nothing negative about this."

"You mean this is nice?"

"It's so nice it's painful." And he smiled at her. "Don't you feel the pain?"

"Yes," she said. "It's a terrible pain. But it's wonderful."

"Where's it got you?"

"All over. Every part of me."

"It's the real thing, all right. No two ways about that. It was bound to happen, it just had to happen. And now it's a permanent state of affairs. We got something here that we'll never lose, not even when we die."

"Don't talk about dying."

"It can be talked about. It isn't important now. It's just a thing that happens to the skin and bones. And what's happened to you and me is way beyond that."

"Yes," she said. "That's right. But please, let's not talk about dying."

"All right," he said. "We'll switch to something else. Let's talk about music. You like the sound of mandolins?"

"If you do."

"So that takes care of that. And from there we go to the moonlight. You like to see the moonlight pouring through the trees?"

"Yes, I like that very much. I'm seeing it now."

"Sure, we're both seeing it. We're getting awfully artistic, aren't we? Let's see what happens if we try another direction. Some topic that has to do with science, like airplanes."

"We're flying now."

"Yes, we sure are."

"We're way up, way way up."

"You hear the motor?"

"No," she said. "Just the mandolins."

Then it was quiet but he heard the mandolins and he looked at her and phrases from sonnets floated through his mind. What he actually saw was a small skinny girl with a face that was fairly pleasant but not especially pretty, although the grey-violet eyes were something unique, and the black hair had a soft lustre that they try to get on canvas and sometimes almost get it but not quite.

But he wasn't seeing her with his eyes. It wasn't her face and body he was seeing. It was something she sent to him, something he'd been waiting for through all the years of listless nights and meaningless days.

He started to say something. He was stopped by the voice from upstairs. It was Frieda, yelling to him, "I'm waiting, Al. I'm waiting for you."

There was a long moment of nothing at all. It was on the order of falling off a cliff.

Then he heard Frieda again. "Come on, Al. Come upstairs."

He closed his eyes and put his hand to his forehead.

"You coming?" Frieda yelled.

Good Christ, he said to himself.

"You better answer her," Myrna said.

"All right," he murmured. And he called to Frieda, "I'll be right up."

"How soon?" Frieda yelled.

"Couple minutes."

"Don't make it longer," with some affection in it, and some warning.

He sat there looking at the stairway and hearing Frieda's footsteps returning to the bedroom. Then he heard the door closing up there, and he blinked hard several times and waited for Myrna to say something.

But she didn't say anything and he knew she was waiting for him to speak.

He said, "I'll hafta go back to that room."

And of course that wasn't enough—it needed more telling, so much more.

"It's a ticklish situation," he said. "She has something on me. If I don't do what she says, she'll talk to Charley and then it's the end."

"All right," Myrna said.

"You know it isn't all right."

"It's all right with me," she said. "Anything you do is all right with me."

"But not that."

"Yes," she said. "Even that."

He lowered his head. He said, very slowly, "God damn it."

"Now look," she said. "I can take it. I'm telling you I can take it."

He looked at her. "Thanks," he said, really meaning it. "It's awfully nice of you to say so."

She smiled. "It ain't no trouble at all. It's so easy to say nice things to you."

"Oh thank you. Thank you very much."

"Don't mention it," she said.

"All right." And he was walking slowly toward the stairway. "We'll cater to society and call it unmentionable. From here on in it's classified tabu."

She didn't say anything.

He was on the stairs and he wanted to look at her, but he knew there was no point in that. And besides, she wouldn't want him to look at her right now. It would only make things tougher for her.

So the only thing to do was continue up the stairs, and then walk along the hall toward the door of the bedroom where Frieda was waiting.

He opened the door and saw the lamp was lit. Frieda was sitting up in the bed and smoking a cigarette. She shifted slightly to make room for him, then gestured for him to get into the bed.

But he walked on past the bed, going slowly toward the window overlooking the backyard. He looked out the window and saw the blackness of Germantown at half past four in the morning. He thought with an inward shrug: Well, the picture can't be any blacker than it is in here.

He heard Frieda saying, "You gonna get in bed?"

"All right." But he didn't move.

"Whatcha doing?" she asked.

"I'm just standing here thinking."

"About what?"

"You'd be surprised."

"Would I? That's nice. I like to be surprised."

"I'm thinking how convenient it would be if I had a bottle of knockout drops."

"For who?"

"You."

"That ain't no surprise," she said. "I figured you were thinking something like that."

He turned slowly and looked at her. He didn't say anything.

She said, "I knew it when I heard you walking up them stairs. The way you came up, so slow and heavy, like an old junkman when he carries too much weight on his back."

"I could make a pun on that," he murmured. "Except that it wouldn't be funny."

"You're damn right it wouldn't be funny." She sat up straighter. "I weigh exactly one-fifty-seven. That's too much weight for you, isn't it?"

"Let's not get statistical."

"Another thing," she said. "You're one of them educated people. I never made it past the ninth grade."

"That doesn't prove anything."

"The hell it doesn't," she told him. "It proves I didn't need schoolbooks to get the brains I got." She tapped a fat finger against the side of her head. "I got plenty in here."

"Really?" he murmured. "Then let's discuss Schopenhauer."

Her eyes narrowed. "You getting fancy with me?"

"I'm getting philosophical," he said. "I think we could use some philosophy at this point."

"You know what? You better come outta the trees."

"But it's nice up here. It's very pleasant."

"That ain't what you mean." Her eyes were narrowed almost to slits, giving her fat face a piggish cast. "You mean it's clean up there. That is, it's clean compared to this bed."

"So now we're on hygiene?"

"Don't," she said. "Don't stretch it too far." Her voice was a mixture of menace and pleading. "You keep stretching it, it's gonna break."

He shrugged. "I didn't start this."

"Not much you didn't."

There was a chair near the window and he sat down in it and looked at the floor.

He heard Frieda saying, "You started it when you heard her screaming downstairs and you jumped out of bed. I told you to stay in this room but you didn't hear me. You hadda go down there to see what was happening to her. And then it's Prince Valiant riding to the rescue."

"Make it Moon Mullins. It was more along that line."

"You wish it was." She said it very slowly.

He looked at her. He opened his mouth to build some sort of a denial, but nothing came out.

Frieda said, "I was watching you. I saw the way you were looking at her."

He murmured, "You're very quick to draw conclusions."

"Not when I'm seeing something right there in front of my eyes."

His mouth remained stiff and tight but the corners went up just a little. It wasn't really a smile, it was more of a calculating look, nothing personal in it, the emphasis on mathematics as he tried to figure the odds. But the odds were awfully high, like a very high mountain telling the climber he might as well give up.

But then he saw Frieda's eyes widening, and she was biting the side of her lip. And he thought: She's reading me wrong, she thinks I'm sitting here making plans for a drastic anti-Frieda campaign; could be she's got me listed as one of the one-track-mind lads who move very slowly toward a decision and then can't be swayed from it. So now it's very interesting the way the table turns and she's scared silly I'm scheming to do her in.

He concentrated on keeping that look pasted to his face. He managed to keep it there and saw the slight shiver that passed across Frieda's shoulders. Now the fear in her eyes was definite and acute. Her voice tried to hide it, making the synthetic command, "Don't get any clever ideas."

The thing to do, he told himself, is keep quiet and let her go on guessing and worrying.

"Because you're really not clever," she went on with the camouflage that didn't get across. "If you were, you wouldn't have given Charley that phony story that I saw through. Me with no high school diploma, I'm a hell of a lot smarter than you and I got you in the palm of my hand and don't you forget it."

He made no reply, not even with his eyes. The smile that wasn't really a smile went floating across the room to Frieda and caused her to shiver again.

"Well?" she demanded. "What's it gonna be?"

He looked away from her. Then he made a vague, indecisive gesture, as though to say: There's no rush, I got plenty of time to make up my mind.

"Now look, I'm getting tired," she said. "I wanna go to sleep."

"That sounds practical," he murmured.

She beckoned. "Come on get in bed," saying it quickly and matter-of-factly as though the other matter was shelved.

He shook his head.

"Whatcha gonna do?" She spoke a trifle louder. "You gonna sleep in that chair?"

"I won't be sleeping," he said. "I'll just sit here and think for a while."

She tried a light laugh and missed with, "Well, I guess you got plenty to think about."

"True." And he nodded solemnly.

"But don't let it throw you," she advised with a forced grin.

He watched her as she pressed her cigarette into the ashtray and put the ashtray on the floor. Then she reached toward the lamp to cut off the light. Her fingers took hold of the cord and she started to pull it, then let go and said, "I think I'll sleep with the light on."

Then she looked at him and he knew she was waiting for a comment. He made no comment.

She said, "Some nights I like to sleep with the light on."

He shrugged. "Suit yourself."

"Another thing about me," she said, "I'm a very light sleeper. The slightest noise wakes me up."

"They sell pills for that."

"I don't need them kind of pills. It ain't like not being able to sleep." She said it slowly and sort of arranging the words to make it a defensive weapon that covered all territory of possible assault. "It's just that I'm a restless sleeper, and if I get waked up all of a sudden I start to yell."

"That's a bad habit."

"Not all the time. Sometimes it comes in very handy."

Golly, he thought, she's really scared, she looks like she's freezing with it.

She lowered her head to the pillow and pulled the sheet and blankets up to her shoulders. Then very slowly she turned over on her side. Her hand came up to her face, and made a careful maneuver that brushed the platinum blonde hair away from her closed eye. Or maybe that eye wasn't closed all the way. He told himself to quit looking at her, and maybe she'd fall asleep and he could begin to think with no one watching him. It needed some proper thinking now, and the important thing was solitude. Or solitaire, he thought. It'll have to be solitaire, and that's one game you can't cheat or bluff, it's got to be played straight, so straight that it hurts. So it isn't a happy game and you're in for a bad time playing it. There's no getting away from it, it's going to be you dealing the cards to you, and naturally that includes Myrna. This one life you got has two people in it now. That makes it a load you're carrying. And that feminine half is precious material, it's a package marked fragile and please be careful, mister. I'm begging you, mister, please be very careful the way you deal these cards.

He sat there in the chair near the window and waited for Frieda to fall asleep. Some minutes passed and her breathing became heavy with the slumber rhythm. It occurred to him she might be pretending, and he shifted the chair so that its legs scraped the floor. But the noise did not reach her and he knew she was really asleep. Another thing he knew, it wasn't true she was a light sleeper, like she'd claimed. What he saw there in the bed was a fat blonde sound asleep, a chunk of sleeping animal that had no connection with him. So now he felt the solitude and he told himself to start thinking.

And where do we begin? he asked himself. What's the jumping-off place? Or let's forget that for the moment and try to figure where we're headed. Referring to the two of us, the girl named Myrna and the man named Hart. If we try to leave this house, it's a sure bet we'll be stopped. But just for the sake of argument, let's assume that Myrna and Hart can negotiate a getaway. Then what happens? The Law happens, that's what. The Law moves in and we're finished. That makes two patterns that offer no exit. Is there another pattern? There better be. And make it more definite than that, say to yourself there's got to be a way out of this, keep saying it and for Christ's sake try to believe it.

But what you're doing here is looking for a short cut, or

giving yourself a head start. And that's a privilege you don't get in this game. According to the rules you got to start from scratch, and that means New Orleans. You'll have to start with your brother Haskell and the way you killed him and your reason for killing him. The method was simple enough, it was a bullet going into his brain. And the reason? That wasn't so simple. It was euthanasia and that's never simple.

In plain words, it was a mercy killing and whether Heaven has it listed as right or wrong, you'd do it again under the same conditions. Because the conditions were unbearable for Haskell and every day he was allowed to live was a hideous session that had him weeping and begging it to stop. But of course it wouldn't stop.

It was a family of snakes crawling through the nerves of his body and eating him up.

It was multiple sclerosis.

And even though the medics are agreed it can't be cured, even though they come right out and admit it's a horrible sickness, they gotta go along with the First Commandment. But you did what he wanted you to do, what he pleaded for with the groans that you can hear yet.

Because you knew he would do it to himself if he could. He told you so. And wept it from eyes that could barely make me out, it's a sickness that hits the eyes as well as other parts of the framework. So he couldn't see where to search for a vial of poison, or a breadknife to use on his wrists. And even if he could see, he couldn't move in that direction, his legs were dead.

And his arms were dead. And his hands, and his fingers.

God yes, it sure had him. All his boyhood and young manhood he'd been the athletic type; at Tulane he won three letters. He was five-eleven and weighed two-twenty and it was packed solid. And a brain, too. And looks. With the kind of personality you don't come across very often. The genuine kindliness, carrying it so far sometimes that people took him for a sucker.

He had an awful lot of money, an approximate estimate would be around three million. And you were next in line to inherit it. So according to the District Attorney the motivation is cash. And in court you stand no chance at all of getting off, and even if some fluke took place and they erased the cash motivation, the law they got against euthanasia is a rigid law and at the very least you'd get seven years.

Seven years for what? All right, don't get sour. It isn't their fault. But God damn it, there ought to be some way to see a thing for what it is, not what Law says it is.

Law calls me a heel and a louse and a murderer. Law says here's a party who did away with his own brother. And the newspapers jump on the wagon and call me worse names, like fiend and demon and dig up stories about how generous Haskell was to me—how he gave me a car and a yacht, and look how I repaid him.

Truth is, he gave me the gifts because he enjoyed giving. I didn't want that automobile and sure as hell I didn't need that yacht. But I drove the car and I sailed the boat and made out I was overjoyed. And that made Haskell happy. It always gave him happiness when he could bring joy to people, whether it was his younger brother or some panhandler on Ransome Street.

You see a man like that, a big fine healthy man with a wholesome yen for living and giving, a man whose only enemies were the envious, a man who was Grade-A clear through, and Mother Nature plays this trick on him. One morning he wakes up with a funny heavy feeling in his left leg.

That's the way it starts, and from there on there's nothing can be done, it gets the leg and later it's both legs out of commission, both arms, the snakes in there multiplying to strangle this and strangle that. He sits there in the wheelchair and you wheel him to the bathroom. And then it gets to the point where the wheelchair is too much for him, he can't sit up. So now he's in the bed and he's getting the weeping spells. You never saw him weep before. In the hall you talk to the doctor, the twentieth or thirtieth in a long line of doctors. You remember this one flew in all the way from Seattle. He sighs and shakes his head and says, "It's hopeless. This multiple sclerosis thing, it's a hellish proposition—" And then, before he can pull it back it comes slipping out, "He'd be better off dead."

It was a statement coming from the mouth of a specialist

in the science of keeping people alive. He didn't want to say it, he didn't mean to say it, but he said it.

So you hear it and it's the seed of an idea going into you and staying, and growing. You try to smother it but that same day you hear Haskell saying, "I don't want to live—"

And some days later he says, "You want to know something? Whenever I go to sleep I pray I won't wake up."

"That's no way to talk," you say. "You got to fight this thing."

"With what?"

"Now look, Haskell. You're going to get well. They'll discover something. They got people working on it. They're bound to—"

"I'm tired, Hart. I'm so tired."

You look at him there in the bed. He weighs exactly one-twenty-seven. You think of the three-letter man from Tulane who weighed two-twenty, the discus thrower who came in third in the Southern Conference championships.

One night a week or so later he puts it to you straight. He says, "I want you to do me a favor."

"Yes?"

"I want you to kill me."

You don't say anything. You can't look at him.

"Please do it," he says. "Please—"

But then the nurse comes into the room with the tray and while she starts feeding him like an infant gets fed you walk out quietly. You go out of the mansion and while you walk around the grounds, past the tennis courts and toward the dock that overlooks a moonlit Mississippi, you're thinking. It would be merciful—

But no, you say to yourself. You can't do that. That's unthinkable.

Except that you can't let Haskell suffer like this, you can't stand by and watch him wasting away.

But listen now, they might really discover a cure. Let's hope and pray. Let's picture them working with the microscopes and the test tubes—

But you don't get that picture. It fades out and all you see is Haskell in that bed, not able to move.

You went through night after night of sitting alone and drinking and really swilling it down but not getting plastered, the alcohol washing all non-essentials out of your brain, all the average-man rules and regulations that state it's a crime, it's the worst sin of all, you mustn't do it, friend, you'll be sorry later. Your reply was: The hell with what society thinks, he's my brother and he needs relief and there's only one way to bring him relief.

Now then, here's a creepy angle. During all this time of coming to that decision but somehow unable to go through with it, the same decision had been reached by your other brother Clement. And that was a surprise, that really knocked you flat. For Clement was never much of a participant in family matters. Fact is, Clement never participated in anything requiring a plus of effort. He was strictly for the hammock and staying home nights with his wife and three children, getting fat and getting bald and the only thing that ever seemed to worry him was his golf score. But Clement was making many visits to the mansion, and for hours he'd sit at the bedside and read to Haskell from *Town and Country,* and *Fortune,* and *Holiday,* and the sports pages of the local newspapers. Then one night you're out on the grounds looking at the tennis courts and thinking of the tennis that Haskell liked to play and would never play again, and Clement comes up and gives it to you blunt and fast, no preliminaries.

Clement says, "I'm going to put a stop to this."

You look at him. You don't say anything.

"The way it's going, it's ridiculous," he says. "It's absolutely ridiculous he should have all that agony."

He says it quietly and sort of tonelessly, and you know he's been giving this a lot of thought.

You hear him say, "I've made up my mind. I'm going to get him out of it."

You wince. This can't be Clement talking.

"I'm telling you and only you," Clement says. "Tomorrow I'm buying a gun."

"Don't talk like an idiot."

"I'm buying a gun and I'm going to shoot him."

"You realize what you're saying?"

You see him nodding slowly and solemnly. And he says, "I'm going to shoot him and then I'll turn myself in. I don't care what they do to me."

"Oh look, you're just talking. Why don't you go home and get a good night's sleep?"

"I haven't had a good night's sleep in three months."

"Why don't you go on a trip? Now there's an idea. You need it, Clement, you need a change."

He smiles. You've never seen him smile like that before. It's the kind of smile they wear when they volunteer for a rescue mission that gives them very little chance of coming back.

He shakes his head. "You can't sell it, Hart. You might as well quit trying."

He stands there, slowly shaking his head, his eyes telling you he's bound to this, it's a sacred vow he's made to himself and there's no way to pull him away from it.

That is, unless—

Unless you move in first and beat him to the punch.

Your brain spins with the thought and you scarcely pay attention as he walks away. You think of this sacrifice he's decided to make, the loss of his status as solid citizen, the ruination of his home, the doom he's bringing upon himself and his wife and children.

But of course you won't let him do it.

From that moment on it's all mechanical, your legs are like wheels on tracks headed straight ahead. You go to the four-car garage and climb into your pale blue Bugatti and some twenty minutes later you're in that particular section of New Orleans where the late-night action is fast and frantic yet somehow on the quiet side because it's mostly illegal trade. In less than a half-hour you've made a connection and the man sells you the gun.

As you drive back to the mansion your hands are steady on the wheel.

You do it very quickly, and there's no strategy, no caution. You go into Haskell's room and he's sleeping. You take out the loaded gun and shoot him twice in the head. As you leave the room you see the nurse coming down the hall and she comes faster and asks you what that noise was. You look at her as though she's asked a foolish question, and you answer, "I shot him."

Then it occurs to you that now you're a fugitive and you'd better start to run.

Jesus, it's been a long run. It's really been no rest for the weary. And the thing that's kept you going and allowed you to live with yourself was the jury inside you, which says, "Not guilty" because what you did was not for cash, not for any personal gain, oh certainly not for that. But even so, it paid off rather nicely for your brothers. It took Haskell out of his misery and it took Clement away from catastrophe. That makes it all right.

Yeah, that makes it just dandy. You better stop rationaliz-ing and come back to these cards on the table, these soli-taire numbers and pictures that you can't argue with, can't re-arrange. All you can do is look at the set-up and see it for what it is.

And what you see most clearly now is the time element that announces today is Thursday and tomorrow is the black day when you step over the line from amateur to pro-fessional. It's gonna be strictly professional up there in Wyncote at the Kenniston mansion. And you damn well better do everything correctly. All right, stop worrying, it isn't Friday yet, you've still got Thursday to brace yourself and develop a purely pro viewpoint.

So let's say that now the only factor is cold cash, that is, the cash is important because travel takes currency and maybe with some luck it'll soon be travel for you and her, to a place where they'll never find you. That kind of travel needs an awful lot of money but I think your share of the Kenniston haul will more than cover it. You're only doing what you gotta do to stay alive and hold onto this girl.

The thought of her was very soothing and relaxing. He closed his eyes and his head went down. He was falling asleep.

Thursday was like the final day for a fighter in training camp, where it's mostly a matter of resting the muscles and the nerves. They sat around in the living room, lis-tened to recorded music from the radio and played cards. There was very little talk and the atmosphere was calm and soft and almost amiable. None of them made mention of what had happened last night.

Supper was a noisy meal but the noise came mostly from the radio. They had it turned on loud and the disc jockey played a lot of Dizzy Gillespie. They sat there and devoured the tender-tasty veal cutlets while Dizzy's trumpet went up and up, going up so fast and hard that you wanted to look up to see if it was puncturing holes in the ceiling.

After supper there was more poker and then they were all in the living room listening to the radio and there was no talk at all. At eleven-thirty Myrna said goodnight and went upstairs. Some twenty minutes later Rizzio went up, and Mattone followed soon after. Now the radio had switched to classical music. It was a program devoted to the works of Debussy. Charley commented it was very nice music. Frieda said, "It sure is." They looked at Hart and waited for his opinion. He was very far away from the Debussy but when he saw them looking at him, he managed to nod in agreement.

It was one-ten when Charley went upstairs. The Debussy music stayed on for another fifteen minutes. Then it was a news program and Frieda went to the radio and switched it off. She stood there at the radio, looking at Hart who sat on the sofa gazing at the floor.

Some moments passed, and then she said, "Come on, let's go up and go to bed."

He didn't respond.

"Come on," she said. She moved toward the stairway. She ascended a few steps and stopped and stood there waiting.

He told himself he mustn't move and he mustn't say anything.

She put her hands on her hips. "Now look," she said, "you got a big day tomorrow and you need sleep."

It gave him a chance to reply and he said, "Yes, I know. That's why I'm going to sleep here."

"There? On the sofa?"

He nodded. "I want to be sure I get some sleep."

She was quiet for a long moment. Her hands fell away from her hips and hung limply at her sides. When she spoke, her voice sounded tight and sort of twisted. "Aw, please," she said. "Please—"

He looked at her. He wondered if she was crying. It seemed the mascara was wet and yet it wasn't dripping, he knew she was trying hard to hold it back. "No," he said.

Then it started to drip, a thick mixture of mascara and tear drops. She lifted her hands to wipe it away but couldn't quite manage the effort. A heavy sigh started from deep inside her and became a sob. She tried to stifle it, choked on it, and then ran very fast up the stairs.

Hart took off his shoes. Then he removed his jacket, arranged himself prone on the sofa resting sideways, placed his jacket over his shoulders, and closed his eyes.

The sofa was fairly soft and he was quite comfortable. In a few minutes he was sound asleep.

In the morning it began to snow around ten-thirty and then it came faster, the flakes swirling wildly, caught in the cross-current of cold wind coming from two rivers. It looked as though it would build and become a blizzard. But gradually it died down and by noontime it had stopped altogether. Then later there was a spell of that unaccountable Philadelphia weather, an acute change that brought warm air from somewhere, melting the snow in the streets and the icicles on the tree-branches. The warm air lasted until late in the afternoon. Around four-thirty it became very cold again, and Charley told Rizzio to put some coal in the furnace.

When Rizzio came up from the cellar, Charley had the card table set up in the middle of the living room. Mattone was lighting a cigarette and Hart was shuffling the cards. They played poker until suppertime, and after supper they resumed the game. At a little after eight Charley said they could play for another hour or so and then it would be time to put aside the cards and get started with the plans.

"What time is it now?" Mattone asked.

Charley glanced at his wristwatch. "It's twelve minutes past eight." Then he added, "Twelve minutes and forty seconds."

Rizzio looked at his own wristwatch and said, "I got eight-fifteen."

"Set it back," Mattone said. "Set it back two minutes and twenty seconds."

"I can't set the second hand," Rizzio said. He was turning the winder of his watch.

"Take it off your wrist," Mattone murmured. "Throw it away."

Rizzio frowned. "Throw what away?"

"Go on, get rid of it," Mattone spoke a trifle louder.

"It's a cheap watch and you shouldn't have bought it in the first place."

"All it needs is regulating," Rizzio said.

"Your head needs regulating," Mattone told him. "Look now, you gonna get rid of that watch?"

Rizzio looked at Charley. "Tell him to cut it out."

"No, I won't tell him," Charley said. "I've told him too many times already. I'm tired of telling him."

"The watches gotta be checked exactly," Mattone said. "If it ain't split-second it means mistakes."

"You're the mistake," Charley said.

Mattone opened his mouth, almost said something, then measured the look on Charley's face and inhaled deeply to hold back whatever he wanted to say.

Charley looked at Hart. "Deal the cards."

They played for about two hours with Hart winning over four hundred dollars and most of it was Mattone's money. Mattone was betting clumsily and his lower lip looked raw where he was biting it. On the next play, he called Hart on what appeared to be an obvious bluff and Hart showed him a third ace that beat his three kings. Mattone gripped the edge of the table and stared up at the ceiling.

"Stop that," Charley said.

Mattone continued to stare at the ceiling. He said aloud to himself, "There's gotta be a reason—"

"For what?" Charley leaned forward, studying the look on Mattone's face.

"For such rotten luck," Mattone said. And then very slowly he got up from the table. For some moments he walked in aimless circles. Then he moved toward the sofa where the newspaper was scattered. He picked up a section of the newspaper and Hart looked at Charley and knew what Charley was thinking. They both knew that Mattone was looking at the dateline.

Then Mattone let go of the newspaper. It went down past the edge of the sofa and drifted onto the carpet. He was looking at it and talking to it without sound.

"Come over here and sit down," Charley said.

Mattone didn't move. But his head turned very slowly and he looked at Charley and said, "You know what day this is?"

"I said sit down." Charley's voice was a whisper that whistled. "We're playing poker."

"It's Friday the thirteenth," Mattone said.

"So?" It was Rizzio.

"Bad luck." Mattone stared past the faces at the cardtable. "Very bad luck."

"Only for idiots," Charley said.

"Charley—"

"No."

"Charley, please—"

"I said no."

And then Mattone cried out, "I'm begging you, Charley. You gotta call it off. We can't do the job tonight. We go there tonight, we'll run into grief—"

Mattone's voice was very loud and it brought Frieda in from the dining room where she'd been sitting with Myrna, the two of them reading movie magazines. Frieda had her magazine in her hand and she was frowning and saying, "What's the matter? What's the matter here?"

"It's Friday the Thirteenth," Mattone shouted.

"He wants we should postpone it," Charley said.

Frieda looked Mattone up and down. She said to Charley, "He looks like he's flipping."

"He'll be all right," Charley said, smiling.

Frieda walked out of the room. Charley went on smiling at her back as she returned to the dining room. Then he gave the smile to Mattone, and he said, "I'm ready to talk plans."

"Look, Charley—"

"You gonna join this conference or you wanna be out of it?"

Mattone took a very deep breath. He shut his eyes tightly,

his body rigid for a long moment. Then he shook his head spasmodically. He took another deep breath and said, "I'm all right now."

"Sure you're all right," Charley said. "I knew you'd be all right."

Mattone came back to the table and sat down. Charley reached into the inner pocket of his jacket and took out the folded paper that showed a diagram of the Kenniston mansion in Wyncote.

"Now here's what we do—" Charley began.

Then he spoke for close to two hours. He outlined the plan in a general way, then went over it again. And then again and again, so each time he got it more detailed, with every move verbally blueprinted. And when he was finished he sat back and waited for questions but there were no questions because everything was clear and it was really a brilliant plan.

"All right, then," Charley said. "So I've told you and now you'll tell me. You first, Rizzio."

Rizzio repeated the plan. And then Mattone. When it was Hart's turn, he heard himself saying it almost word for word the way Charley had said it. The words came out automatically, like a recorded recitation.

"Very nice," Charley said. He glanced at his wristwatch. "Well, it's time to get ready."

The four of them got up from the table.

It was ten minutes to one.

They were putting on their overcoats. Mattone and Rizzio wore dark brown camel's-hair and Charley's coat was a midnight blue chesterfield. Hart was buttoning the bright green fleece and he could feel the heaviness of the cheap fabric on his shoulders.

He turned and faced the door of the vestibule so he wouldn't see the light in the dining room where she sat with Frieda and read the movie magazines. He wanted very much to see her and talk to her and tell her she mustn't worry, that everything would be all right. But seeing her now would be bad for both of them, awfully bad. And he thought: She knows it, too. That's why she's staying there in the dining room.

Then he wondered why Frieda also remained in the dining room. It didn't take much guessing and his brain said: Well, it's certainly no picnic for Frieda. She's torn between her need for you and her hate for you. Her need says she wants you to stay alive, and the hate wants her to come in here and hit back at you for what you're doing to her. Or what you're not doing. You sure did some damage to her last night.

Yes, all she needs to do now is come in here and tell Charley you're not fitted for this job, you're not a professional. But there's nothing you can do about that. All you can do is hope for Charley to open the door so we'll be out and away before she makes up her mind.

He saw Charley moving past him and opening the vestibule door. Then the front door was open and the four of them filed out and went down cold steps onto a cold pavement. The January wind came at them and it was terribly cold.

"It's freezing out here," Rizzio said.

"All right," Mattone said. "So it's freezing. So shut up, will you?"

They were walking now at medium stride, Charley and Hart walking in front, with Charley setting the pace. At the corner they turned and went south on Tulpehocken. There were cars parked on both sides of the street, packed in close, almost bumper-to-bumper. Toward the middle of the block they arrived at their car and it was a 1951 two-door Plymouth sedan. It was painted black and looked older than it was, it hadn't been washed for some time.

They climbed in and Mattone sat at the wheel, Rizzio beside him. Charley and Hart settled themselves in back.

Mattone hit the starter. There was the sound of the starter but no engine. Mattone hit it again and the same thing happened.

"What's wrong?" Charley asked.

"It's cold," Mattone said.

"Got anti-freeze?"

Mattone didn't answer. He was trying the starter again. The engine turned over and made an effort and then died.

Charley sat up a little straighter. He said very slowly. "I'm asking you something, Mattone. Does it have anti-freeze?"

Mattone turned and looked at Charley. "Yes, Charley," he said, his mouth stretched wide with the words jetting out through his teeth. "You told me to put in more anti-freeze and I put it in."

"All right," Charley said. "Try it again."

Mattone pressed the starter and this time the engine caught and stayed alive. Mattone gunned it and it became very much alive. Hart heard the extra power and he knew it was a souped-up engine.

Now the car was sufficiently warmed and Mattone nosed it out from the row of parked cars and took it north on Tulpehocken to Morton, then west to Washington Lane, then north again to Stenton. At Stenton there was a red light and a red police car parked at the corner. There were two policemen in the front seat and one of them was reading a newspaper under the glow of the streetlamp. The other policeman was looking at the Plymouth.

"What's he looking at?" Rizzio wanted to know.

"Shut up," Mattone said. And then, hissing it, "Quit looking at him. For Christ's sake, will you stop looking at him?"

The policeman leaned his head out the car window and said, "Hey you."

"Me?" Mattone called back.

"Yeah, you," the policeman said.

"What's the matter?" Mattone asked.

"Dim your lights," the policeman said.

"Sure, officer." Mattone dimmed the headlights. "Sorry, officer."

"Remember, you're still in the city," the policeman said now more politely. "Keep them headlights dim until you're on the highway."

"Yes, sir," Mattone said. "Thanks, officer."

The signal light turned green and they turned left on Stenton, stayed on Stenton and passed the wide road going north toward Wyncote. There was some teen-age Friday night traffic on that road and Mattone was looking for a narrower road. He found it about a mile further up. It was bumpy and in sections it was unpaved but the Plymouth had good tires and they held their grip nicely.

They came onto another road that was new and smooth, going past blocks of brand new road houses. Then they turned onto a curving road, going north past large homes. As they continued north, the houses kept getting larger and larger with wider lawns, then fenced-in properties with private roads leading to the mansions set far back from the highway. The car went up a steep hill and on the downgrade it moved slowly past an iron gate that glimmered like black teeth in the glow of the headlights. The iron gate went on and on and now the road was level again and the car moved very slowly. They kept going past the gate for another quarter of a mile and then Charley said, "Stop here."

"Here?" Mattone asked.

"Right here," Charley said. "Stop the car."

The car came to a stop at the side of the road. Charley told Rizzio to get out and switch the license plates. Rizzio opened the glove compartment and took out a screw driver and a license plate and got out of the car. Rizzio did it very quickly and when he came back with the plate he'd replaced, he flipped the screw driver into the glove compartment, then slid the plate into a groove behind the wall of the compartment where it would not be visible to anyone who might be obliged to see what was in the compartment.

The engine was idling and Mattone put the car in gear and they went along the road at around fifteen miles per hour. There was another hundred or so yards of iron gate and then some fifty yards of high stone fence belonging to the same estate and then the wide entrance of the private road.

Mattone turned the car onto the private road. It was a winding road bordered with high trees. They went along the road for the better part of a mile, and then there was the small house of the caretaker coming up in front of the headlights. One of the windows was dimly lit and as they approached the house, a side door opened and a man with white hair stepped out and walked toward the slowly moving car.

Mattone stopped the car and the old man stopped also. He stood about twenty feet away from the car. His old man's voice sounded sleepy. "What do you want?"

"We're going to Doylestown," Mattone said.

"Not on this road," the old man told him.

"Why not?" Mattone asked. "Ain't this the way to Doylestown?"

"This is private property," the old man said.

"Oh," Mattone said. "I guess we made a wrong turn."

"You sure did." The old man stood there with his hands at his sides.

"Say, how do we get out of here?" Mattone asked.

"Just turn around and follow the road."

"I mean, how do we hit the main highway going north?"

"Well, what you do is—" The old man walked toward the car. He was ten feet away from the car and then five and Mattone opened the door and got out. The old man said, "You gotta get onto Old York Road. That's the shortest way to Doylestown. And what you do is—"

Mattone hit him with a short right to the jaw and caught him before he went down. Then Rizzio was out of the car and they put the caretaker in the back seat. He was unconscious and he was sprawled between Charley and Hart, his head resting on Hart's shoulder. Hart glanced at the face and saw it was a very old man with an opened sagging mouth that showed false teeth.

The car was moving again and they went along the winding road going past a greenhouse and a Japanese garden and the two-story structure that was the servants' quarters. Then up ahead in the moonlight there was the white marble of the Kenniston mansion. Now the headlights were off but the mansion was distinct in the moonlight.

It looks more like a college library, Hart thought. Then he heard the groan and he glanced at the face of the old man. The old man's eyes were open and the lips quivered with consternation and outrage and fright.

Charley was talking to Mattone, leaning forward and pointing to some shrubbery about forty feet away from the side-entrance, saying, "Park it over there near them bushes." Then he turned to the old man and said, "What's your name?"

The old man was very frightened now and he couldn't talk.

"Come on, Grandad," Charley urged softly. "It ain't that bad. Just tell me your name."

"Thomas—"

"How old are you, Thomas?"

"Seventy-three."

"Aw shucks," Charley said. "That ain't old."

The old man closed his eyes and said quietly, "It's too old for this kind of business."

"Don't worry, Thomas. You'll make out all right. All you gotta do is pay attention and do what I tell you."

Then Charley took the the gun from his pocket. The old man opened his eyes and saw the gun.

"Now listen to me very careful," Charley said, holding the gun loosely but with the muzzle pointing toward the old man's abdomen. "You're coming in with us. If anyone comes downstairs and wants to know what's happening, you'll tell them we're from City Hall, we're detectives."

The old man blinked several times. "Detectives?"

"Yes, we're detectives and someone tipped us off there'd be some action here tonight, a couple ex-cons coming to break in and grab them oriental treasures."

"That's what you want me to say?"

"No, I'll say it. What you do is make out you're in Hollywood, you're a high-paid actor. You nod your head in agreement, you tell them we showed you our credentials and we're really detectives."

"But I'm not an actor," the old man said. "They'll see I'm scared clean out of my wits and—"

"You won't be scared," Charley told him. "You'll be thinking how nice it is to be alive and stay alive."

"All right," the old man said. "I'll do my best."

Now the car was parked near the shrubbery. Mattone and Rizzio climbed out and walked toward the mansion, and Charley said to the old man, "You see how we play this game? Them gentlemen are the two ex-cons. They're the bad guys and we're the good guys. When they break in we'll be staked out, we'll be there to get them."

Hart watched Mattone and Rizzio walking slowly along the side of the mansion. He saw Rizzio moving ahead and crouching in dog-trainer fashion as two large Doberman pinschers came loping across the lawn. The dogs slowed down and Rizzio didn't move as the dogs walked up to him. Hart couldn't hear anything but he knew Rizzio was talking to the dogs. Then Rizzio was patting the dogs and they didn't seem to mind.

"I wonder how he does it," Charley said.

"He better be careful," the old man said, momentarily forgetting his own fright and feeling afraid for Rizzio. "Them dogs are awfully vicious."

"Not now they ain't. Look at them."

The dogs seemed very friendly. They were rubbing their noses against Rizzio's legs. He went on patting them and talking to them.

"It's remarkable," Charley said. "He never misses. I think he has some dog in him."

Rizzio was walking the dogs, holding their collars, and Mattone followed at a distance of about thirty feet. Then Rizzio turned and beckoned, and Mattone came in closer. Hart watched the merging of the four figures now silhouetted against the whiteness of the Kenniston mansion. He saw the two men and the two dogs moving past the rearside entrance, and then at the rear of the mansion they turned the corner and went out of sight.

Charley glanced at his wristwatch. He said, "We wait two minutes."

"There's a light on upstairs," Hart said.

"I see it," Charley said.

"It just went on."

"No," Charley said. "That's an optical illusion you get when you first see a lit window. I saw that light about a minute ago."

"It wasn't lit when we got here," Hart said. "None of the windows were lit."

"All right, don't worry about it."

"I'm not worrying," Hart said.

"You sound like you're worried," Charley said.

"You want me to tell you what I think about all this?" the old man suddenly asked.

"Sure," Charley said, "tell me."

"Well, mister, I got the feeling you won't get what you're after."

"Thanks for telling me," Charley said. "Now I'll tell you something, Thomas. I want you to get rid of that feeling. I want you to feel you're working with this crew and we're gonna do this job and do it right. You understand what I'm saying?"

The old man nodded.

Charley brought his wristwatch toward his eyes and murmured, "Fifty-eight, fifty-nine—two minutes." He opened the car door and climbed out facing the old man. Then the old man climbed out, and then Hart. The three of them walked toward the side entrance. On the doorpanel there was a large mother-of-pearl button and Charley pressed it. A few moments later he pressed it again. He was pressing it a third time when the door opened and a middle-aged man wearing a bathrobe stood there and stared at them.

"We're the police," Charley said.

So then it was up to the old caretaker, and he nodded and said to the middle-aged man, "It's all right, Mr. Kenniston. These men are detectives from City Hall, and—"

"Come in, please." The middle-aged man moved aside to let them enter. In the hallway he switched on a light, and they followed him into a large room that had a Chinese motif. It was all ebony furniture and rose-quartz lamps and vases of delicately carved jade.

The middle-aged man was facing Charley and saying "Will you kindly tell me—"

"I'll hafta tell it fast," Charley said. "We're here to prevent a robbery. We got a tip. It might be happening at this very minute. I mean, they might be on the grounds right now, trying to break in. Or maybe they've broken in already. So you see we gotta move fast. There ain't time to do much explaining."

"But—"

"Look, mister. You got something very valuable in this house. You got a collection of oriental antiques worth maybe a million. We got it listed in our records, it's our job to protect that kind of property. But if you wanna lose it, that's up to you."

"But I don't understand why—I mean, you could have phoned—"

"We can get them with the goods this way."

The middle-aged man was frowning at the floor. The frown was more thoughtful than worried. For a long moment there was no sound in the room, and then all at once some sound came in from somewhere in the rear of the mansion. It was a mingling of footsteps and the scraping of chairs, and the middle-aged man gasped, "What's that?"

"It ain't mice, that's for sure," Charley said.

The middle-aged man became pale. "Why don't you do something? What are you waiting for?"

"I'm waiting for you," Charley said. "I can't protect your merchandise unless you tell me where it's stashed."

Then it was quiet again and the middle-aged man was biting his thumbnail. And Hart thought: It's gonna be yes or no, and what's it gonna be?

The middle-aged man said, "Please come with me."

Charley looked at Hart. "Wait here." And then he was following the middle-aged man across the room. There was a large ebony-paneled door at the far end and they were halfway to the door when something went wrong.

It started with the dogs. Hart heard the growls and then a scream from the rear of the house, the sound of glass crashing, a table overturning, and now the screaming was terrible and the growls were noises from very bad dreams.

The middle-aged man said happily, "The dogs got them."

Charley looked at Hart and didn't say anything.

Hart heard the sounds coming nearer and then a shoulder hitting a door. He turned and saw the door giving way, and Rizzio running in very fast with a Doberman pinscher flying after him and landing on his back. Rizzio went to his knees and the dog had its mouth opened wide to bite into his neck. The look on Rizzio's face was acute puzzlement, his eyes seemed to be saying: How could this happen? I know how to handle dogs.

Charley reached into his overcoat pocket and took out the gun. He shot from his waist and the bullet went along a path maybe two inches away from Rizzio's face, hitting the face of the dog, hitting it between the eyes.

The dog rolled over dead and the middle-aged man shouted at Charley, "Why'd you do that?"

Charley didn't answer. He was looking at Rizzio. And Rizzio looked back at him and said, "I'm sorry, Charley. I—"

"Charley?" the middle-aged man said it slowly and quietly. "Oh, so that's it. You're working together."

Charley shrugged. He moved the gun so that it covered the middle-aged man and the old caretaker. But now there were more sounds, a mixture of footsteps and voices from upstairs, and a feminine voice calling anxiously, "What is it, Merton? Are you all right?"

"Yes," the middle-aged man called back. "I'm quite all right, my dear."

"I'm coming down," she shouted.

"No, don't do that." The middle-aged man said it loudly but calmly. "Just lift the phone and call the police."

Charley smiled wearily at the middle-aged man and said, "Now why'd you hafta tell her that?" He moved the gun just a little so that it was pointed at the chest of the middle-aged man. "You see what you've done? Now it gets sloppy. I hate when it gets sloppy."

Without sound Hart said: Don't, Charley. Don't do that. And then he saw the old caretaker running in to shield his employer, lunging at Charley with both arms raised high. As Charley pulled the trigger, Hart moved in very fast and hit his arm. The bullet went into the carpet. The old man made a grab for Charley's hand holding the gun, and Hart gave the old man a shove and sent him to the floor.

Charley looked at Rizzio. "Where's the other dog?"

"I don't know—I guess—"

"You guess," Charley said. "I thought you knew all about dogs. You're an expert with dogs."

Rizzio sighed. He shook his head slowly.

"Come on," Charley said. "Let's get out of here."

The three of them backed out of the room, Charley's gun covering the middle-aged man and the old caretaker until they were in the hallway. Then they walked to the side-door and out of the mansion. As they crossed the lawn, headed toward the parked Plymouth, Rizzio was pointing and saying, "There's the other dog. Over there, Charley. You looking?"

"No," Charley said. "You look."

"Aw, don't, Charley. Don't be that way."

"What way?" Charley asked mildly. "I'm just telling you

to look, that's all. I want you to have a good look."

"Jesus," Rizzio said. And then he sobbed it. "Oh Jesus—"

And Hart was looking and seeing the broken window, with the Doberman standing under the window at the side of his prey. In the moonlight the body of Mattone was very white where his flesh shoved through his ripped clothes. His clothes were almost entirely ripped from his torso. He was resting on his back, his chin tilted up at an acute angle, showing all that had been done to his throat. Much had been done and there was little of his throat remaining.

They were getting into the Plymouth. Rizzio slid in behind the wheel and Charley said, "Get a move on. There's gonna be red cars here in a few minutes."

Hart leaned back against the rear-seat upholstery. He heard the engine starting, he felt the car moving. It moved fast going across the lawn onto the private road. On the road and headed toward the highway bordering the estate, it was hitting fifty on the curves. Then later, on the highway, it was hitting eighty and eighty-five and ninety.

They were on a narrow street in the West Oak Lane area when Charley told Rizzio to stop the car and get out and change the license plates. A few minutes later they were in Germantown and the car moved slowly past red cars. There were a lot of red cars around and the policemen were looking at all small black sedans that drove past, and checking the plates with the written numbers they had in their books.

The car came onto Tulpehocken, going very slowly into its parking place in the row of closely parked cars. They got out and walked north on Tulpehocken toward Morton. On Morton the wind came screeching at them and it was like the blast of a trumpet going up very high.

Want some coffee?" Frieda asked.

"No," Charley said.

"It'll do you good," she said. "You could all use some coffee."

"All right." Charley was sitting on the sofa. He was still

wearing his overcoat and muffler and hat. Rizzio and Hart had taken off their coats and they were sitting in armchairs on the other side of the room.

"I'll make it good and strong and you'll drink it real hot," Frieda said. "It'll do you the world of good."

Then she walked out, going toward the kitchen. The three of them sat there and Charley began to unbutton his overcoat. He freed one button, then the next one, and then forgot about the third. He began to fumble with his muffler, got it halfway off, and let go of it and pressed his hands flat and hard against the sofa pillows.

Rizzio said, "I'm trying to put it together and see how it happened. I just can't understand how it happened."

"It's all right," Charley said. "Forget about it."

Rizzio was quiet for some moments. Then he said, "You know what I think? I think there was something wrong with them dogs."

"Do you hafta talk about it?" Charley asked softly. "Can't you let it drop?"

"I had them dogs under perfect control," Rizzio said. "And then, for no reason at all they get agitated and start all that hell. Or maybe—"

"Maybe what?"

"Maybe there was a reason," Rizzio said.

Charley leaned back against the sofa cushions. He folded his arms. He looked a question at Rizzio.

And Rizzio said, "The date, Charley. Friday the thirteenth."

Then it was quiet.

Finally Rizzio said, "What about it, Charley? You think I got a point there?"

"I'm playing with it," Charley said. He looked at Hart. It was the first time he'd looked directly at Hart since they'd come back to the house. He spoke very softly to Hart, saying, "What's your opinion?"

Hart shrugged. "It wasn't Friday when we made the try. It was after midnight, so that makes it Saturday morning. This is Saturday the fourteenth."

"He's right," Rizzio said.

"No, he's wrong," Charley said. "It's still Friday the thirteenth." And he went on looking at Hart.

Rizzio frowned and scratched the back of his head.

Charley said, "It's Black Friday and for certain people it's a day that never ends. They carry it with them all the time. Like typhoid carriers. So no matter where they go or what they do, they bring bad luck."

"Meaning me?" Hart murmured.

Charley nodded slowly. Then very slowly he reached into his overcoat pocket and took out the gun.

"What's all this?" Rizzio said. "What's the matter, Charley? What are you doing?"

"He's getting superstitious," Hart said.

"That's part of it," Charley said. There was no tone or color or anything in his voice. "The other part is, you're not in our bracket, you can't work the way we work."

Hart shrugged again. He was looking at the wall behind Charley's head.

He heard Charley saying, "What it amounts to, you're not a professional. I found it out when the old man jumped at me and you hit my arm to ruin my aim."

Hart smiled. He knew there was no use arguing the issue. He said, "I guess that did it."

"It sure did," Charley said. "With that one move you gave yourself away."

And Hart thought: So this is the way it usually happens. It doesn't need a Frieda to spill the beans. Sooner or later we do it ourselves, we give ourselves away.

Then he heard himself saying, "Can I ask a favor?"

"Sure," Charley said. "You can ask."

"I'd like to see Myrna."

"Myrna?" Charley's eyebrows went up slightly. "Why Myrna?"

Hart didn't answer.

Charley went on looking at him for some moments, then looked at Rizzio and said, "Go upstairs and wake up Myrna. Bring her down here."

Rizzio got up and headed for the stairway. From the kitchen Frieda was calling, "Coffee's ready," then calling it again some moments later, and finally coming in to see why they didn't answer. She saw the gun and she said, "What's this?" And Charley said, "He's going."

"What?" She whispered it. "What?"

"I said he's going. He's gotta go. We can't use him."

"Oh," Frieda said. She looked at Hart. She saw he wasn't looking at her. His eyes were focused on the stairway. There were footsteps in the hall upstairs, then Rizzio was coming down, and then Myrna.

Charley was looking at Frieda and saying, "He asked me to do him a favor. He said he wanted to see Myrna."

Frieda took a step toward Hart. "Damn you," she said. "God damn you."

He didn't hear that. He lifted himself from the arm-chair, smiling at Myrna as she came down the stairs. She wore a white satin quilted robe. Her hair fell loosely onto her shoulders, the black strands lustrous against the white fabric. Her eyes were bright, fully awake, so he knew she hadn't been sleeping. He knew some-how that she couldn't sleep because she'd been thinking about him.

And now for a very long moment there was no Charley, no Frieda, no Rizzio. It was just the girl and himself, look-ing at each other, their eyes saying things that couldn't be said with the spoken word. They stood a few feet apart but he felt her presence very deep inside himself. It was a fine feeling.

He heard Charley saying, "You wanna talk to her?"

"We're talking," he said. But then he knew the talk was ended because Myrna had turned her head and she was looking at Charley and the gun.

Hart thought: Well, maybe I can tell her a lie and maybe Charley will back me up. He said to her, "It's all right, there's nothing to worry about. It's just that Charley is sending me away for a while—"

"That's right," Charley nodded.

But it was no good, it didn't fool her. She went on looking at the gun.

And then there was a laugh. It came from Frieda. It was the closed-lip laughter of negative thinking, negative enjoy-ment. Frieda let it out and breathed it in, savoring it. She said to Charley, "Do it now, while she's here. I want her to see this."

"No," Charley said. "There's no point in that."

"The hell there ain't," Frieda told him. "Go on, do it now."

"You keep quiet," Charley said. He sounded tired and gloomy.

Frieda made a gesture of frantic impatience. "I'm telling you to—"

"You're not telling me anything," Charley said. "I told you to keep quiet."

Hart wasn't listening to that. He was measuring the distance to the vestibule door. The door was halfway open and he estimated it was less than five feet away. He told himself it was near enough and there was nothing to lose, he might as well try it. He looked at Myrna and her eyes said: Of course you'll try it, you gotta try it.

Frieda was saying, "Shoot him, Charley, shoot him. What are you waiting for?"

"Can't you keep quiet?" Charley said it slowly.

Hart lunged for the vestibule door. In the same instant Myrna threw herself across the path of the bullet coming from Charley's gun. Hart had not yet reached the door and as he saw her going down he lost all interest in getting past the vestibule.

She rested face down on the floor. There was a hole in her temple and a thin stream of red came out and formed a pool on the carpet.

For some moments none of them did anything or said anything. Then Rizzio walked toward the body and knelt beside it and felt the wrist.

"She's gone," Rizzio said.

Hart looked at the corpse. But then his eyes were closed and he was seeing inside himself and she was there.

"Pick it up," Charley said to Rizzio. "Take it down the cellar."

Rizzio lifted the small skinny corpse and carried it out of the room.

Charley was looking at the bloodstains on the carpet. He said to Frieda, "I don't want that there. Get some cleaning fluid—"

"I'll do it in the morning," Frieda said.

"You'll do it now."

"Why can't I do it in the morning?" Frieda whined. "Jesus Christ, I'm all played out."

"So am I," Charley said. And then he sighed. "I think it's caught up with me."

It was quiet for some moments and then Frieda gestured toward Hart and said, "What about him? Whatcha gonna do with him?"

"Does it matter?" Charley murmured. The gun was loose in his hand and it wasn't aimed at anything. "Does it really matter?"

Frieda frowned. "What is it, Charley? What's happening to you?"

Charley didn't answer. His shoulders drooped and his head went down low. The gun fell out of his hand and dropped over the side of the sofa onto the floor.

"Charley—" Frieda went to the sofa and sat down beside him. She put her arms around him and pulled his head down to her bosom.

"I'm so tired," Charley mumbled. "I'd like to fall asleep on a train going away—away—"

"Poor Charley."

"Yeah, you're right. That's what it all comes down to. Poor old Charley."

Frieda looked at Hart. Her voice was lifeless. "Put on your overcoat," she said. "Get out of here and don't come back."

"Oh, let him stay," Charley murmured. "What the hell's the difference?"

"No," she said. "I don't want him here."

The bright green coat was draped over the stairway railing. Hart took it and put it on and walked out of the house. As he came down off the front steps onto the pavement he remembered the money he'd won in the poker game, telling himself there was more than four hundred dollars rolled up in his trousers pocket.

And maybe that'll help, he thought.

But somehow it wasn't an important thought, and after some moments he let it fade. He was walking very slowly, not feeling the bite of the cold wind, not feeling anything. And later, turning the street corners, he didn't bother to look at the street signs. He had no idea where he was going and he didn't care.

About the Author

David Goodis was born in Philadelphia in 1917. The
publication of *Dark Passage* in 1946 established him
as a leading author of crime fiction and after the success
of the film, starring Humphrey Bogart and Lauren
Bacall, he joined the Warner Brothers payroll as a screen
writer. His collaboration with Hollywood was less than
ideal and in 1950 he returned to Philadelphia and
continued to write crime fiction until his death in 1967.